A NEW KIND OF COUNTRY

Dorothy Gilman

FAWCETT CREST • NEW YORK

A Fawcett Crest Book
Published by Ballantine Books
Copyright © 1978 by Dorothy Gilman Butters

Library of Congress Catalog Card Number: 77-12852

ISBN 0-449-21627-6

Manufactured in the United States of America

First Ballantine Books Edition: April 1989

Contents

A New Kind of Country

> The main problem is no more whether there is
> life after death but whether there is life after
> birth.
>
> —PROFESSOR ALBERT SZENT-GYORGYI,
> NOBEL LAUREATE

 THIS IS ABOUT LIVING IN A FISHING VIL-
lage in Nova Scotia, and it's about living
alone, and about being a woman alone.
Thoreau remarked in the opening pages of *Walden*, "I
should not talk so much about myself if there were
anyone else I knew so well," but this is not about myself, not really. It's about discovery. We're collectors,
each of us, for all of our lives, collecting years, illusions, attitudes, but above all experience, and to me it
seemed very simple: I wanted a different kind of experience.

I was tired when I made the first hesitant decision:
of the war in Vietnam that went on and on with accelerating violence; of inflation, which alarmed me; of
being a single woman in the suburbs, which seemed to

me a slow death of the spirit; of being always in a hurry and never having enough time for anything. To this was added a quite blatant unease: after raising two sons by myself for ten years, the younger one was soon to go off to college and I would face an unemployed heart.

Once, when I was very young, there had been a kind of scenario, never quite defined, which had grown out of dreams and hopes and the tender assumptions of the young. I would be a writer. I would go to far places and have adventures. I would build a tiny shack in the woods and raise herbs and bees.

Very tender assumptions. I wrote stories lovingly that no one believed in, least of all my parents, who felt it kinder to discourage than encourage. The bees and herbs I could read about, and did, in book after book. There was a shack in the woods near the lake to which we traveled each summer; I observed it and coveted it year after year, but it was occupied by an old man who started his wood fires with kerosene and one day burned up both the shack and himself. The distant places I collected carefully on paper, hanging maps on every wall of my bedroom.

The one item not in my scenario was marriage, which happened along before anything in my life had been put together, and following this I was whisked off to the hinterlands with the pressing need for a caring someone fulfilled, but the need for myself tucked away in the dark recesses of a locked closet. I had been, after all, a fragile person and my dreams had been just that.

But these constants remained: a writing of stories and books, and the devout feeling that all of us must grow inside or die, that it's given to us to live, not on a straight line but a line that slants upward, so that at the end, having begun at point A, we may have reached, not Z, but certainly an ascension to I or J. Both of these constants were my undoing and there came a day when, taking two children with me, I left marriage and staggered back to life, very unlived, very frail, very unsure and anxious, to begin life all over again.

And to spend the next years in growing up, coping with problems and stresses, cheering Little League games and seeing Disney films, traveling both with my children and alone, with an occasional peek into that dark closet in which was housed the small dreaming child that had been myself.

One of my most prized books when I was that child had been John Cowper Powys' *Philosophy of Solitude*, already an old book when I met it at the age of nine or ten in the library. I don't think I read it through completely, or even understood it, but something in me must have recognized even as a child that we are born alone and we die alone, and that we'd better learn how to handle aloneness, and solitude. The book was like the map of a country I'd caught only glimpses of, but I knew it was a country rich in flora and fauna, as well as tricky ravines and cliffs and—oh, yes—the abysses. I already knew something of those abysses; the therapy

I'd had at the breakup of my marriage had pointed up the legacy of frail underpinnings I'd inherited and the longings for security that had drawn me too early to shelter. Insecurities are not cured overnight: I might have dreamed of distant places, and by now have visited a dozen foreign countries, but I'd had anxiety attacks in every one of them. What I suffered from, I knew, was a terror of what Paul Tillich calls Non-Being, the big emptiness, the fear of disappearing literally into the void without people nearby to reassure. But Tillich had written about this in a glorious book called *The Courage to Be*, and I insisted on "being." Of mattering—at last—to myself. Without props. Cold turkey.

And so I chose Nova Scotia, I don't know why, because I'd never visited it before in my life. But it was another, gentler country, it was accessible to the United States by ferry or plane, and I could buy land on the ocean for a tenth of what was possible in the United States. What my sons and I found on that first visit, two years before I moved there, were ten acres on the water facing a lighthouse, and an elderly house with six small rooms and no bath, all for the price of $10,500.

Two Septembers later, a week after Jonathan left for college, I moved into that house, which had been half gutted, a bath placed in the pantry, and the six dark rooms turned into two large sun-filled spaces. I had no passport for this new life except a number of books on raising herbs and vegetables organically, a patch of garden that Clarence Amiro had backhoed for me two months earlier, and a longing to convalesce from some nameless disease which, for want of any better definition, could be called civilization or Society.

2

The Beginning

 FOR THE SUM OF $10,500 I HAD RECEIVED ten acres "more or less," as the deed phrased it, of earth, rocks, fern, wild blueberries, blackberries, raspberries, wild primroses, an incredible number of wildflowers, and, down near the beach, cranberries that glowed like red jewels in the fall. These ten acres included a large barn that stood very near to the road, and a 125-year-old house at the end of a long drive. Beyond the house the land began a long gentle slope down toward the beach— but not so gentle when pushing up wheelbarrows filled with seaweed—first through wild mallows, then primroses and wild irises down to a belt of ferns, and thence to the damp mossy bog with its cranberries until—suddenly—one was at the beach.

Mine was a lovely, wild, and primitive beach, with nothing polite about it. There were boulders—harsh, rugged boulders—on which one could climb and stand. Its floor was cobbled, with small flat rocks the water had worn smooth, and tufts of salt grass growing up between the cobbles. The shore faced a beach pond, a sheltered body of water which the receding tides left flat and green as a billiard table. But just beyond my property line, off to the left, the beach took an abrupt and spectacular turn and ran out into the harbor in the shape of a long curving finger that formed the opposite shore of my beach pond and supported the lighthouse, which had once been a handsome affair of wood and shingle, with people living in it, but was now a kind of Erector Set structure whose housekeeping chores were divided among a computer and two lightkeepers who lived in matching houses nearby. Beyond the lighthouse lay the harbor, which would be busy with lobster boats in their season, and beyond this the open ocean.

And so from the one side of the house, looking west, I could see lighthouse, harbor, and ocean. The sun set behind the lighthouse each night, trailing plumes of color across the pond; the beam from the lighthouse flashed regularly across my walls at night, and in fog the foghorn sounded, or bellowed, or moaned, depending on the direction of the wind and clearness of the air.

From the north windows I looked out upon fields of alder and blueberries, and a solitary railroad track down which, once a day, puffed the little train that brought freight and groceries to the village.

From the east window I could see the highway, and the houses and lights of my two neighbors, the Nixons and the Crowells, while on the south side lay garden, well, a field, and the matching lighthouse keepers' cottages on Lighthouse Road.

A great deal had been included in the purchase price; I had actually taken lien on a small universe. And to this universe, besides books and clothes and furnishings, I brought all my suburban ways of thinking, and made an enthusiastic attack on the particular when it was the general that needed attention. I flailed away at inconsequentials. It was early September when I arrived but I rushed to get ready for the herb garden I would plant in the distant spring. I made trips to the lumberyard in town—a distance of thirty miles each way—and brought home expensive boards, which I cut and nailed to form artistic shapes for planting boxes. It was incredibly obtuse of me. It didn't occur to me that I need only walk out to the lighthouse, and somewhere along that stretch of Far Beach I would find all the boards I could possibly use, as well as wooden barrels washed up by the storms, and bait boxes and lobster crates with hinged lids, and enough lumber to build a house. Like a horse wearing blinders, I looked and admired but from a distance, without relationship, my concentration fixed upon lists: paint deck, bring up loads of seaweed for garden, buy pegboard, nails, trowels, hang curtains, fill kerosene lamps, locate bales of hay—and each day during those first two months the sun shone radiantly, the temperatures remained balmy, the piles of seaweed in the garden grew thick, and my lists grew longer and more tyrannical.

Until one day something stirred in me, and walking into the kitchen to cook breakfast I looked out at the harbor and the ocean and at the sun slanting through the windows and I kept walking through the door and out of the house into the eight o'clock fragrance of a soft October morning.

There is an incredible luminosity to the light in Nova Scotia, a southern Mediterranean quality on a sunny day that astonishes the eye with its unexpectedness. The sun reaches the earth without smog, it glances off rocks and water, turns the sky a vivid blue and the water, reflecting it, is sapphire or cobalt and glitters under the sun until it floods the senses. Forgetting breakfast, I turned into the path leading to the beach, found my shoes drenched with dew, hesitated, half turned to go back and look for boots, and then impatiently stripped off my shoes and continued down the path barefooted. Each mallow leaf I passed held a drop of dew in its hollow center that looked—as the sun set it afire—like a diamond dropped there during the night. The grass was rough as rattan on my feet, and wet. When I reached the shore my feet ached with cold and I climbed up on a rock to warm them before I ventured on the beach.

It was low tide, and when the tide retreated it had left water and sea life behind it in small hollows and crevices. I found periwinkles clinging to the rocks, minnows in small ponds, empty clam and mussel shells, and long brittle ropes of kelp. There was a thick fragrance of salt in the air, and of rich decaying muck. When I turned to go back, something strange had happened. The sun, not high enough yet in the sky to flood the shore with light, was just illuminating a long row of rocks along the shore. Each rock was densely covered with seaweed, and in this juxtaposition—of soft golden light and long slanted shadow—the rocks looked like human heads wearing outrageous wigs of tangled hair . . . a dozen heads in a row staring primly out to sea . . . a line of gossipy ladies nodding in the sun.

I laughed out loud.

And standing there laughing on the beach in the morning sun, I felt the rigidities inside of me—the inhibitions and timidities and shoulds and oughts and musts and schedules and routines and tensions—as iron bands that encircle a barrel and hold it together by pressure.

It was startling; it was frightening; it was revelation.

I put on my shoes and scurried back up the hill to breakfast.

But it was a beginning.

3

The Village

 A Nova Scotia village is very nearly an enclosure. In passing it may look like only a few houses scattered along the road with a church, a general store, and a post office, but there is an intense, hidden life and a deep sense of community.

In the village where I lived, which I shall call East Tumbril because that isn't its name, there were only a few defined professions: the priest, the carpenter, the electrician, the postmaster. Skills were handed on or self-taught, interwoven and cross-sectioned in a neighborly sharing way. The carpenter, for instance, rarely went beyond the village to work; he was taught by his father and is teaching his own helper now, who happens to be his brother, and his brother may remain a

11

carpenter or help another brother who goes lobstering, and so veer off in that direction. This provides a permanent job pool that's based on family, friendships, and eclectic skills. Clarence, for instance, is one of the kingpins of the community but it would be hard to precisely define his role. He owns earth-moving equipment: a backhoe and trucks. He has a gravel pit, he digs basements, takes rocks out of gardens and occasionally works on the roads for the government, and has been known to supply firewood. He sometimes goes lobstering, too.

To have a field plowed, one calls Frank, who plows only because he cares about his village: he has a mink farm—2,200 minks at last count—and two cows and a huge garden. He charges so little for plowing that it's embarrassing: only gas money the last time, and that had to be pressed upon him, "because the earth's still so damn wet I couldn't do a good job." Frank likes to do a good job.

Running through this tapestry—the most colorful threads—are the lobstermen, who supply drama and temperament for the land-based villagers, and who, when not fishing, do not usually spread their talents: they hunt instead, or race snowmobiles like warriors on holiday. But they provide herring to their neighbors in the fall to be salted away in barrels for the winter, and will arrive at one's doorstep with a bucket of lobsters as a gift. Their life is hard and they know it.

The first year I was there, in the next village up the road, seven men were lost at sea. The captain rounded up six men to test out his new fifty-foot secondhand trawler and they sailed out of the harbor with the radio not properly tested yet and were never seen or heard of again. An explosion at sea, the Coast Guard reluctantly concluded months later. But when a lobster pot is being dropped into the sea with the winch running tight and fast it's been known to take a man to the bottom of the sea with it, or pinch off a finger or an arm if a man isn't alert. A lobster pot is heavy, and weighted with stones to carry it fast to the bottom, and it's quick, precision work. Two men go out in each lobster boat, the owner and his helper, called a "nubbin," and the boats generally go out in pairs, too, so that if the wind comes up and the weather turns foul or an engine breaks down, there's someone nearby to help. Sometimes they work inside the harbor, but more often they travel a long way, perhaps twenty or thirty miles out, where a change in wind can pit them against waves twenty feet high.

Trawlers are bigger and go farther and stay out longer but they're herring men. Audrey's brother-in-law has a trawler, and there were three days during a wild storm when no one could raise him on the ship-to-shore radio until at last someone out on Cape Island heard his faint voice saying his radio batteries were weak but he was okay and heading home. The word was passed along from village to village, radio to radio, until it reached his wife.

Such a sense of community spills over into the village to become the warp and woof of its life. These are deeply rooted people, and few leave. It has its drawbacks as well as its advantages. Privacy is not a pre-

cious commodity and there is very little that anyone
doesn't know about his or her neighbor, whether true
or not, and the mores are strict. Not abided by, necessarily, but firm and difficult to circumnavigate. The
girls usually marry young, and it's not uncommon to
find a twenty-year-old with four children. A wife with
a car of her own, even if it's an old jalopy, is regarded
with some suspicion: she's considered "independent."
The only jobs available for women are in the fisheries
in the summer, where the wages are very low. There
are few secrets and many rumors; I've had a number of
people, male and female, sit across the kitchen table
from me and say, "I can tell you this because you're
from outside; there's nobody I could say this to here, it
would be all over the village in an hour. . . ."

To a person arriving from the "outside," however,
there are some pleasing aspects to this after years
spent in cities where one could die in June and nobody
notice until Christmas. Not long after moving to East
Tumbril, but long enough to have established a pattern
of my lights going out at eleven, I went to bed one
night at ten-fifteen. Some ten minutes later the telephone rang and it was Vaughn Nixon across the road.
Bill had been dreadfully worried, she said, and had
begged her to call. Had my lights gone out early because I was sick? Was I all right? Did I need anything?

I assured her that I was fine, just tired, and went to
bed a little startled but chuckling. It was as if I had
moved into a village of invisible lines crossing and
crisscrossing to provide a network of support. And it
was a network, as I came to realize over and over

again. Perhaps this was why I never felt any unease at living there alone, which surprised me, because as a child I'd been afraid of the dark, and with the sort of imagination I have I can turn innocent shadows into monsters.

But perhaps, too, it was the incredible silence of the nights, into which an alien footstep would scream its arrival, a silence uninterrupted unless for the foghorn on a foggy night, or a car passing. I would turn out my lights at bedtime and look out of the window in my living room and when there was moonlight, no matter how faint, I could see the path's black shadow cutting a wound through the long grass, and then I would glance across the harbor and far off to my right I would see the lights of West Tumbril, another fishing village, with its red and green wharf lights followed by a long chain of white lights reflected in the black water.

And then of course from the opposite window I could see the Nixons' house. "When I go to bed," Bill would tell me, "every night I look to see if your lights are still on."

That's simply the way it is in East Tumbril.

4

Weather

DURING THE TWO BRIEF PERIODS WHEN
I visited East Tumbril before moving
there, I would ask everyone I met about
the winters. Not cold, they told me, not really cold at
all, certainly never below zero. What about snow? I
asked. Not much, they said, and never a real storm
until January. It seemed too good to be true, because
my friends in New Jersey seemed to believe that I'd be
snowbound for half the year.

There had to be a catch, I thought, and continued
asking.

The first clue came only two months before I moved
in, when Jonathan and I drove up to Nova Scotia to
start a garden and see if the heat had been put in; it
came at the local diner three miles down the road.

Talking with the owner, I asked again about the winters.

Not cold, the woman told me, not really cold at all.

Snow?

Not much.

"Good heavens," I said, "it sounds even more temperate than New Jersey."

"Well," she added as an afterthought, "we do get some wind."

I had found the catch.

My first taste of wind came early in October. The sun shone brightly, the wind blew from the southwest, and there were certainly no signs of storm, but I woke in the morning to find the beams of the house creaking and complaining like a sailing ship on the high seas, and when I opened the kitchen door a giant hand flung it wide, taking me with it. It wasn't particularly cold, but although the thermostat in the living room was set at seventy degrees the temperature kept sinking ominously; for the first time I questioned its story-and-a-half ceiling. Outside, clouds scudded across a blue arc of sky, whitecaps raced, the seaweed I brought up from the beach had to be weighted down with a stone, but I felt healthy and hardy as I practiced leaning against the wind, all but tumbling to the ground when the wind suddenly slackened.

After three days the wind abated, leaving only a faint memory.

On November 1 I drove into town for groceries in a pouring rain, with lightning flashing across the sky. By the time I arrived home again, the sun was shining but the wind had risen and to my astonishment the waves in the harbor were sending spray high up over the Far Beach to actually embrace the lighthouse. This was something new. By eight o'clock in the evening the wind had reached gale force. I sat on the couch facing the window, a book on my lap, and tried not to notice how the couch and the floor trembled under me. A storm door blew open and had to be rescued; beams creaked and groaned; the wind sounded like a blast furnace as it burst around the corner of the house. I reminded myself that the house had stood there for 125 years, and this was comforting until I remembered the beams I'd asked the carpenters to remove, and the extra glass that had been added. The storm grew steadily worse as the winds increased—to 80 mph, I was to learn later. Salt spray blowing against the windows sounded like sand peppering the glass; doors rattled and I could see the picture window trembling under each gust. By ten o'clock the mirror on the wall over my bureau was doing a little dance step, the glass in the windows was shaking, and so was I. . . .

Somewhere in there the phone rang, and it was Vaughn Nixon. "Quite a wind," she said in her mild voice.

"It is, isn't it," I agreed.

"Your barn door just blew out."

"Oh," I said.

"Come over here if you'd like some company."

"Thanks but I think I'd better stay," I said, feeling that without my 120 pounds the house might very well blow away.

"Guess you won't do much sleeping tonight."

"You can be sure of that," I told her, and hung up.

But human nature is perverse; this wind was something new and unknown to me, but one can be cowed for just so many hours. I had assumed that I'd stay up all night and keep the house under me by sheer concentration, but the noise of it all was exhausting and it grew tiresome watching mirrors dance. There came a kind of anger at giving in to it, so that I took a defiant and leisurely bath at midnight and then, feeling braver, climbed into pajamas and then into bed. I turned out the lights. The wind was still seizing the house and shaking it, slapping the roof and the walls with a brutal hand, whistling, then screaming, and at last roaring. It was no longer a graspable phenomenon, it was beyond rationality, it was too enormous to comprehend. "And so," I thought drowsily, "to hell with it," and fell asleep and slept like a child.

The barn door was nailed on again, and doubly secured, not to be blown out again until the Groundhog Day storm of 1976, the worst in a hundred years, but I had been initiated. I learned that a wheelbarrow left outside unsecured could be blown to the opposite end of the meadow overnight. To trace the lid of a garbage pail, carelessly unweighted, I learned to stop and think from what direction the wind had been blowing during the night, and then set out accordingly to track it down. Somehow I always did. I learned to open car doors very cautiously so that the wind wouldn't seize them and rip them off their hinges. I learned how to lean against the wind when I walked. The wind during the winter months was simply chronic, like an asthmatic condition: always present, in varying degrees. In my kitchen on windy nights it adopted a roaring sound as it raced around that corner; if I disliked that sound I could move into the living room, where it whistled.

This also explained Clarence's odd reaction when I asked him, upon my arrival, to please put my driveway on his snowplowing list.

"Well, now," he said gravely, eyes twinkling, "I can't say that'll be necessary."

"You must get snow," I pointed out. "And I have a long driveway."

"Oh, we get snow," he said, nodding, "but I doubt you'll need your drive plowed."

And of course I didn't; only once did I shovel any snow at all, and that was one day when the wind deposited it near my kitchen door, combed it and shaped it into an artistic crescent, and left it for me like a gift package. It snowed, yes, but I never knew where the snow went: it was swept away by the wind to other places, perhaps into the woods or on up to Halifax. Nor did snow ever drift down lazily from the sky, or down at all for that matter; it always snowed perpendicularly, on a slant, dancing across the meadows with the wind behind it.

When we first visited East Tumbril my son Jonathan said, "Have you noticed the way everybody talks about the weather? You'd think there was nothing else to talk about."

Well, in a way there wasn't. The weather was *there*,

an integral part of life, elemental, unpredictable, and always, *always* dramatic. I could leave for town in a thick fog, reach Tumbril Centre to find the sun shining, and drive through a snowstorm before I reached town. When the sun shone it was dazzling, when there was fog it was wraithlike and pearly, drifting past one's windows or sometimes following one up from the beach when it moved in fast; and then of course there was the wind. As I grew immersed in country life I, too, began every conversation with speculations about the weather; what else was more important? Even today I remain uneasy if the day ends without a complicated weather report and a complete marine forecast; I remain eternally braced for the unexpected now, which in East Tumbril was the norm.

5

Time

> God works in moments
> > —AN OLD FRENCH SAYING.

 IT WOULD BE LESS THAN HONEST TO SAY that I embraced a new lifestyle in a new country without innumerable doubts, anxieties, and setbacks. I knew that I had come to East Tumbril because I wanted to, but there were moments when a distortion of shadow gave it a mocking glint. I think women are more prone to doubt because of their history of compliance. Being intuitive by nature and brought up to be a little less than men in the scheme of things, by purest osmosis we pick up signals about what we should and shouldn't do and be. We learn early to please, to be appealing, to say the right things, and to accept injustices. For instance, when I was growing up my closest friend was the eldest of three children and very bright; when the youngest child was born and proved to be a boy there was no dissembling: she knew her education would end with high school and that the boy, less of a student then she, would be the one to go to college. It was simply reality.

In my own family my father's liberation was due, perhaps, to the fact that both of his children turned out to be girls. If you have only daughters, then some rearranging of attitudes becomes imperative and he gallantly, loyally demanded the best for us, but at the same time I knew that I was supposed to have been a boy, and would have been named Theodore if I had been, and although nothing was ever said of marriage being the best and only route for women, my mother's voice would change when she spoke of unmarried women. "X is so very nice," she would say wonderingly, "and really so attractive *that I wonder why she's never married.*" Presumably there had to be something deficient, something flawed there, invisible to the eye like a fruit that looks luscious on the outside but has rot inside. The antenna picks up these signals early.

To be oneself needs first of all self-esteem, and then autonomy, which grows out of self-esteem and is a matter of governing oneself without undue influence and according to one's deepest values. Lacking self-esteem, it's so much easier to be what may be called, for want of any kinder phrase, a soul-snatcher: to live with and through someone else, symbiotically, without thinking of oneself, acting for oneself, or making cold hard decisions for oneself. Life then becomes a study in the art of concealing, placating, influencing, and reacting rather than acting. One sees oneself never directly but through a line of mirrors that reflect back what neighbors, husbands, friends think and feel about us, so that if we're told we're adorable we at once become adorable, or if waiflike we immediately cultivate widened eyes and a waiflike posture, or, if efficient, never, *never* leave dishes unwashed in the sink—and by the time this reflection reaches us it's a graven image and not ourselves at all. Our true selves have been traded for a mess of pottage: for approval, security, safety, and a "you scratch my back and I'll scratch yours and never mind if I think you're a darned fool."

It's hard to separate oneself and stand alone: for a cause, for a belief, for a purpose, even to try something new. And for women the rules are a little more complicated than for men. It's hard enough *physically* for a woman to continue being a teacher or physicist after she's had a child, but emotionally it's hardest of all: she runs the intolerable risk of being called not independent but selfish, or, most biting of all, masculine. Women who do creative work at home have equal problems because there's no uninterruptible time and they're socialized to respond to every household crisis, no matter how trivial. We move from guilt to guilt, damned if we do, and damned if we don't.

One particular day my own uncertainties reached a climax when I'd driven to Barrington Passage to buy groceries. As I drove home I experienced, first of all, an overwhelming sense of—not homesickness—but of not-at-home-ness. Instead of the small cluttered market I'd just left, I longed for an American supermarket with its bright lights, canned music, and gourmet foods. I wondered what on earth I was doing in this country of weather-beaten old houses, lobster boats, and flat terrain; it wasn't *home*. And then I wondered in a spasm of guilt what this was going to do to my two sons, their mother removing herself to such a distant corner for a small adventure in living; would they feel I was rejecting them, abandoning them? Would they still come to see me or would they reject *me*? And following this army of guilts came platoons of doubt: was I perhaps running away from life by coming here, or was I, in moving here, subtly punishing myself in some excruciating Freudian manner? Was I really going to like this? What had I been thinking of to come to a place so alien?

I felt something very like terror. With every fiber of my being I longed for the known, for a face that was of more than several weeks' familiarity; I could feel my sense of what and who I was trembling and then dissolving like jelly underwater. Everything looked foreign, and the anxiety of it—my audacity gone —turned me numb, so that I could scarcely feel at all: alienation had struck. I arrived home, tottered from the car, and put away the groceries. The moving van had not yet arrived with my furniture or with the desk that is a constant in my life; my typewriter sat on the kitchen table and it was the only familiar thing in sight. I sat down at the typewriter, shivering, and I thought, "I'll sit here all day if necessary, I won't move an inch." And I sat there for a very long time until I began to see the ludicrousness of it, and after that I went out to call on a neighbor and felt better.

But of course the same doubts and anxieties came and went through all the early months. The first snow flurries abruptly ended two months of blissful sunny weather and brought a new gray season; I felt a sense of loss and then of anxiety over what might come next, for change is what anxiety is all about.

But being here in East Tumbril I had the time to think about such matters and get to the bone of them, and one day I suddenly understood the root of my malaise. You could take all the ups and downs, the uneasiness, the dismay, and the anxieties, shake them up and they'd still fall into one slot. What I suffered from—at bedrock level—was a fear of freedom.

My life had become as spacious as the sea that stretched to infinity beyond the window, and almost as uncluttered. Like so many women, I had lived first of all with my parents, and then with roommates at school, then with a husband, and finally two children, and so I had never lived alone before; it had a strange taste to it. There were no demands being made upon me or my time. I could, if I wanted, stay up all night and sleep all day, learn Russian, take a lover, play the phonograph at ear-bending volume, or be anything I wanted to be.

It was a country I'd never visited before. It was this that was foreign, not my surroundings.

And it was frightening.

And yet, knowing the name of the demon now, I could begin the work of banishing it. When I looked around me and thought, "I've finished this and finished that, it's raining, and what am I to do with all this time?" I would sniff scornfully and say, "Aha—afraid again?" I would pull on my boots and raincoat and walk down to the beach to jump over rocks or to look —*really* look—at its treasures, or—most astonishing of all—do nothing, and find it companionable. How we race to avoid empty time!

It's strange that one of the dictionary's definitions of the word "empty" is: *to remove from what holds or encloses*.

And one of its definitions of the word "freedom" is: *not bound or confined or detained by force*.

The difference between the two is so small it's embarrassing. It's a matter of adjusting the heart as if it's a watch that gains a few minutes every day. It's learning a new language.

This sense of freeness, of time opening up and out, was to become one of the major discoveries of living there, and if I frequently lost it I grew patient enough to wait for its return. It was not so much a new dimension of time but of me, alive, *within* time.

For time really exists only in our minds, its reality another of our more cherished illusions. Both the clock and the calendar are man-made; it's we who have placed hours in a day and weeks into a month and divided each year by twelve, which was masterful of us, efficient and convenient, but what we call time existed long before man put a frame around it, and will continue to exist if every calendar is banished overnight. Physicists, philosophers, and astronomers have only theories about time; it's still an unsolved riddle. We know we can't measure time, although we try to.

We think time is eternal but no one has ever defined eternity. We live in time but we can't touch it, we occupy it but we can never own it. We speak of killing time, spending time, passing time, consuming time, using time, wasting time, we speak of spare time, the time of our lives, time hanging on our hands, and of losing track of time. Prisoners do time, or serve time. But does anyone know what time is?

All that we can really know of time is inside of us, and for each person it's different, and for each experience it's different. Sometimes time drags, at other moments it races. A minute can be shallow, deep, endless, burdensome, or hold within it all the elements of magic and mystery, so that we have quantitative time, of which so many hours of our lives are made, when life seems dull, changeless, routine, and we have qualitative time, when we do something infinitely satisfying to us, or when something breaks through the shell of our days.

Abraham Maslow calls the latter "peak moments," when suddenly life takes on new meaning and we see it with freshness, a great givingness and joy. Our rigidities melt and we wonder how we ever allowed our lives to become so shrunken. It's as if we've been blind and we abruptly see: a blade of grass, the clouds in the sky, another's face, the harmoniousness of the world.

Yet the mystery is this: that whether we experience time quantitatively or qualitatively, time hasn't changed at all, it's we who have changed. All that's happened is that we've been jolted by events into awareness, into transcendence. Jolted out of routine, habit, complacency, and conditioned thinking. In a sense we have been jolted out of time into living *now*. With wide-open eyes.

Maurice Nicoll writes: "The time-man in us does not know Now. He is always preparing for something in the future, or busy with what happened in the past. He is always wondering what to do, what to say, what to wear.... He anticipates; and we, following him, come to the expected moment and lo, he is always elsewhere, planning further ahead. This is becoming— where nothing ever is. We must come to our senses to begin to feel *now*."*

Nothing in our society teaches us how to live now, everything in our society circumvents it. When we reach school our parents and our teachers are already saying, What Next? Get ready! We enter college and the pressure increases: What Next? We become conditioned early to thinking ahead, and apply it everywhere; it has become a habit of thought. We look ahead to arriving somewhere—anywhere, it scarcely matters. We anticipate the wonderful day when we find the magic "other" with whom life will be so much richer, and then to next year's vacation, or to what we will do when the children are grown, or to retirement. We are always in suspension, and when the future arrives that is to magically heal and change us it turns out to be no different from today.

It is possible—it *has* to be possible—for us to cultivate a different kind of life, to live with more joy and

*Maurice Nicoll, *Living Time* (London: Vincent Stuart, 1952).

awareness, with heightened consciousness, so that we deepen each moment and fill it with content. We pass over moments lightly, our eyes on tomorrow, but it's the present that belongs to us now, and is trembling with possibilities, not the future, which exists somewhere else and hasn't arrived yet. "In stripping time of its illusions," Emerson writes, "in seeking to find out what is the heart of the day, we come to the quality of the moment, and drop the duration altogether. It is the depth at which we live and not at all the surface extension that imports."

It is only when we enter a moment and live it with attention that we become truly alive.

"To die," says J.B. Priestley in his book *Man and Time*, "is not to close our eyes when we come to the end of our lives, but to choose to live in too few dimensions."

6

The Lobstermen

ON THE SOUTHWESTERN SHORE OF Nova Scotia the lobster season begins in late November, with what is called Dumping Day, and continues through late May. Not the happiest of choices, one would think, with January and February too weatherish for lobstering, but the men don't mind: up Halifax way the season runs from June to late November—the other half of the year—and that has its drawbacks, too: the competition's keener, and the lobsters fetch a lower price.

On Dumping Day the rules are precise: no boat can head out to sea before eight o'clock in the morning, and the Coast Guard frequently sends a small, clean-lined white cutter to enforce the rule. By half past seven the lobster boats are lining up around the East

Tumbril wharf, each piled high in the stern with pots, buoys, lines, and bait, their engines idling and waiting. If there's no sign of the Coast Guard, if another village has been chosen for patrol that day, one of the boats will break away early and the others follow en masse. They begin to pass the lighthouse in tandem, while far, far behind them comes the flotilla of boats from across the harbor at West Tumbril, a wonderful serpentine line of yellow, blue, green, black, lavender, white, and red Cape Islander boats heading out of the harbor to the ocean. Once past the lighthouse they begin to spread out so that by the time they reach open water they stretch across the horizon in a long line, while from stage left there emerges a new fleet of boats from the next village up the coast. If it's a gray and sunless morning their white mast lights will glow like pearls on dull pewter.

The boats will be back soon—by midmorning or noon—to pick up a fresh load of pots but not until the next Dumping Day will they be seen so magnificently together. For the rest of the day the harbor will be busy with boats coming and going. Not for a day or two will there be lobsters, for a lobsterman will, at the very least, have four hundred pots to take to sea and dump for the start of this new season.

It's the first week that matters most: it gives an indication of the season ahead, the hauls are largest the first week, and bills have been piling up during the six months on shore. The first day's catch may net a man two thousand dollars, all of which will go toward his twice-a-year payment on his boat, or to his boat's repairs, or the new radar he's installed, or the new engine. The second day's take is by custom divided between the captain and his nubbin; the third day's haul will pay the considerable expense of his gas, oil, and bait. On the fourth day the wind may keep him at home, and always there are the months when he can't go out at all. Yet, if the lobsters keep coming in, and if the harbor doesn't freeze over too early, and if his boat doesn't break down—there are many ifs in the life of a lobsterman—the average yearly gross may be in the neighborhood of thirty thousand dollars.

When the boats begin bringing in lobsters there's no need to be told; it's announced by the great swarms of swooping, diving gulls that accompany each catch. Down at the wharf the boat draws up to the lobster car and the lobsters are handed over to be weighed and packed into crates that float, roped together, in a long line in the water. In return for his haul each man gets a slip of paper; the next day, up at the office, he trades this in for his cash: it's an arrangement based on trust. When he returns each night—four-thirty or five o'clock, usually—he'll gas up and check his boat before leaving for a beer, and in the morning he'll check it all over again. Mistakes at sea are paid for heavily.

Having been given a few early lobsters by neighbors to whet my appetite, there came a day early in December when I wanted more and knew I'd have to make a trip to the wharf to buy them. It happened on a day when it was raining and blowing hard, to which I gave little thought, being a newcomer. I drove down to the wharf, parked my car, and carrying two buckets and a purse, I left the land world behind.

It's a long wharf, with a second wharf running off at right angles to shelter the boats: a businesslike piece of property, stout of beam and plankings and lined with all the accouterments of lobstering. Sea gulls dove and quarreled over the boats that had nosed their way in out of the wind; water lapped at the piles below. I walked past several trucks, piles of lobster pots and ropes, looked down among the boats tying up, and waved to my neighbor Raymond. I turned left onto the second wharf, passed the diesel pumps, and found a man unwinding ropes there. Above the wind I shouted, "Where do I buy lobsters?"

He jerked his head. "There."

"Where?"

"There." And with this he pointed down.

Way down.

Some fifteen feet below the wharf lay the lobster car, a shack built on a square floating platform tied to the piles, and on this day rolling and pitching with each wave that broke over it.

I was new to East Tumbril, and I was "the American"; I knew that something was at stake here. I looked at the lobster car and I looked at the narrow metal ladder descending to it and I was aware of a number of interested faces turning in my direction. I said weakly, "*Right.*" I hung my purse over one arm, strung the two buckets over the other arm like bracelets, and aimed one chancy backward foothold at the first rung of the ladder. The rungs, I found, were wet and slippery and the buckets nearly sent me into the harbor; I hung there, disentangling myself, and hurled the buckets down ahead of me; as I descended rung by rung the lobster car came up to meet me and then plunged with the impact of the next wave; when I reached the platform I was in water up to my ankles. I picked up the buckets and sloshed around the side of the shack to find Tippy Martin weighing lobsters and only a little startled to see me. He picked out four lobsters, weighed them on his scale and took my five dollars: $1.25 a pound that day.

Returning was easier. Hands suddenly appeared to help me over the top of the ladder, and my two buckets, filled with lobsters, followed me up to the wharf on a rope. I shouted my thanks, smiled at Raymond, beamed at everyone I passed, and as I slowly walked back down the wharf, the rain in my face and the wind at my side, I felt that I had passed a major test in flexibility and personhood. I did more than swagger; I swashbuckled.

The life on the wharf never lost its fascination for me and what impressed me the most, besides the smell of salt air and the water lapping against the piles, was the camaraderie among the men. One could feel it and taste it. They were young, all of them; in East Tumbril I never met a lobsterman over forty. They had grown up together, give or take a few years, and all in the same village, and their intimacy was expressed in the nicknames they'd given each other: Wharf Rat, Crazy Raymond, Dormouse, Sweet Pea, Screwie Louie, Sardine, Petit Pop, Grizzly Bear, Juke Box, Weasel, Bogo, Sned.

"There are good days and bad days," Raymond says, "but the thing is, a man belongs to himself out there. I never have to answer to anybody."

For this freedom, for being his own man, a lobster-man heads out to sea at five-thirty or six in the morning when it's still dark, and works for ten or twelve hours hauling his pots, rebaiting them, and dumping them. He and his nubbin will steam out of the harbor checking the sound of the six-cyclinder Ford engine or four-cylinder diesel, moving at eight or ten knots when the engine's wide open, to head for his particular grounds and the sight of his own buoys. The engine slows, he gaffs a buoy and hauls in the slack rope; it's secured to the hoist, the pot rises up to the snatch block, he reaches up, grabs the pot and drops it on the curb, tosses the lobsters into a crate, rebaits the pot, and he's already on his way to the next buoy while his nubbin's dropping the pot back into the sea. Only a minute has passed. For lunch he'll cook a batch of lobsters on the "little cod" oil stove in the cud, and perhaps throw a painter to a nearby boat and have a bit of a gossip with a friend before continuing. He'll wear no gloves in spite of the wheelhouse being shallow and open on one side to the weather, and on some days the wind-chill factor pierces the bone. If it turns rough he'll say it's "breezing up" or "blowing pretty breeze now." For the East and the West Tumbril fishermen the southwest wind is the worst. The colder northwest "takes it down" or makes it "ca'mer."

"I don't guess my son'll be a lobsterman," Raymond says of his year-old boy. "Won't be any lobsters left by then." He adds, "Some nights there are so many Russians out there it looks like Christmas with all the lights. Far as you can see."

Each year there is an erosion in the weight and size of the catches; a lobster needs ten years to grow to maturity and the big floating fish factories send down nets to cull the bottom of the sea and recklessly bring up undersized lobsters as well as herring and haddock. Every year a few generations of lobsters are destroyed. And the independent lobsterman is already an anachronism. The Canadian Government subsidizes them to some extent to keep them going but, like a cottage industry, their efficiency can't match the streamlined fish factories.

And fishing *is* a craft in East Tumbril. Every single pot is made by hand. The wood for the bow is steamed over a wood stove in the garage or basement until it's pliable enough to curve. The cleat, the nuzzle, and the spindle are whittled and carved by hand with a jackknife. Each man knits his own nets that make up the bedroom head or parlor of the pot. There is an incredible craft involved, all of it taken for granted. It's simply part of his work.

By the time April comes around the lobstering has grown easier but following April comes May, when the hauls have dwindled and the season comes to an end. During the last week the boats begin bringing back not only lobsters but empty traps for storing and repairing. The landscape becomes dotted with them: along the road, in back fields, piled up beside the houses. The boats are beached, four or five of them in a corner of the beach pond in front of my house, to be repaired and painted over the summer and fall months, but by this time most of the men will have their minds on "going mossing" if it's a good season for Irish moss. The season that began so dramatically comes to an end gently, almost casually, in a burst of sun and promise of summer. The harbor looks strangely, bleakly empty and except for an occasional freighter or the lighthouse ship bringing in supplies, the glitter on the water is rarely shadowed by more than a passing cloud.

7

Loneliness

 ON ONE OF MY TRIPS BACK TO THE States, this one by car and ferry, I traveled on the ferry with an American fisherman from Port Judith, Rhode Island. By coincidence his new lobster boat was being built in the West Tumbril shipyard across the harbor from my house, and he had come up to see how the work went. We talked about lobster prices, the differences in cultures and government rules, climate and living standards. He was very perceptive, very articulate, and he said of the land we were leaving, "It's incredibly beautiful and very lonely, very harsh."

Harsh yes, unadorned and severe as well, and lonely. But so, I think, is life anywhere that has only been lightly touched by men and commerce. This

shore on which I lived had none of the pleasing soft-
ness of the west coast of Nova Scotia, with its apple
orchards and rolling hills, and so no one had come to
reshape it or change it. Its only commerce was fishing,
and the people were very small against, and near to,
Nature. So it must be, living at the edge of a desert or
very high among the mountains. Everything becomes
clearer, more vivid, because everything is on a one-to-
one basis. Even loneliness.

I would walk to the beach every day—a point of
honor here—no matter what the weather. Sometimes
I would find it wintry and desolate, like a moonscape,
or there would be huge blocks of frozen snow and ice
tossed so high by the tide that only the black tips of
rocks could be seen. Or the shore would be covered
with thick, knotted glare ice with veins of yellow curving through it. For days at a time the beach would be
covered and the rocks buried; under cloud it would
look somber, a frozen surreal volcano's edge, and on
the path yesterday's footprints would have become
fixed until the next thaw. In sunshine it was an expanse
of glittering white, the only color the tawny beige of
dried grass springing out of the snow, and the tender
shadows in the hollows.

And then would come brilliant days in January
when ice would float down the harbor toward the
ocean, and in the sudden warmth I would find tips of
garlic plants coming out of the earth in the garden. In
a southwest wind I could walk on the beach again and
sun myself on a rock, little wavelets making noise
against the shore, and every minute or so I would hear

the distant boom of larger waves against the Far Beach. After rain would come fog, or perhaps a snow that swept so densely across the meadow that it blotted out the lighthouse and the pond.

One evening, walking in from the barn in the cold of an eleven-degree temperature, every star in the sky was etched brilliant above me and the windows of my house were framed squares of light and warmth: a patch of red showing at one window, a vignette of bare wood from another, a corner of the stove in the kitchen. I stopped outside in the quiet a moment and listened to the wind combing the frozen grass—it made a soft, silky, whispering sound—and except for this there wasn't a sound to be heard in the silent night.

There can be a sense of aloneness that is downright voluptuous, a drawing in, a sense of plenitude and delight. And there is a type of aloneness that is austere, disciplined, not happy yet not unhappy either, usually given at moments when we understand that something difficult has to be faced alone, that a unique life experience can't be shared, regrettable and sad as this may seem. And then there is the ragged, harsh, and inconsolable sense of aloneness that is actually grief, I think, and this is called loneliness.

Being alone is not being lonely. Lonely is when your mind begins spinning webs about what's missing, the people or the years that have been lost, or what your hopes have been, the desires you've cherished that haven't been fulfilled; or it's questioning the very meaning of life and seeing yourself as a solitary fly-speck on the face of the earth. It's a deficiency instead of enoughness; it's savage, bleak unhappiness.

Krishnamurti defines unhappiness as the distance between What Ought to Be and What Is. The mind sees...the mind measures...the mind questions... the mind longs for...the mind looks for loss and mourns it...the mind constructs scenarios of what our lives ought to be. "The mind is never still," Krishnamurti points out, "it is in continuous movement... One thought follows another without a pause; the mind is ever making itself sharp and so wearing itself out. If a pencil is being sharpened all the time, soon there will be nothing left of it; similarly, the mind uses itself constantly and is exhausted."*

When there is loneliness and one stops to listen it is interesting to observe that in spite of physical inertia the mind is racing like a small trapped furry animal bent frantically on escape. The mind is trying to solve its dilemma by the very means that trapped it—by thought. Round and round it goes, looking for comfort, never realizing that the twist of the kaleidoscope that shut out life has darkened the mind and the emotions, too. If it was a feeling of rejection that triggered the loneliness, then our thoughts, like a tongue searching out a troublesome tooth, must search out other, older rejections and lay them side by side. If it was doubt that alienated us we begin a laborious analysis that only compounds our sense of worthlessness; if it is loss that seeded our loneliness then we see a future

*Krishnamurti, *Commentaries on Living*, 2nd Series (New York: Quest Books, 1967).

entirely without hope, and thus suffer the loss of hope as well. We stubbornly occupy ourselves with What Ought to Be, and turn on life for denying us.

What *Is*, on the other hand, is to still the mind and to relax . . . to concentrate on the weight of our bodies in the chair, listen to the clock's ticking and to the beat of our hearts, observe how the sun glances off the edge of a table, or watch a bird wheel and drift across the sky. It is to enter the moment, which has no memory. When this happens, when we turn our attention to What Is, there is no longer any room for loneliness, or past, or future, or unhappiness or fear, there is only What Is, and a complete acceptance. It is when the mind has quieted and we have died to those thoughts that were so full of ego and pain that we understand how far away from ourselves we had gone in our suffering, and how imprisoned we'd become. The human mind, which has harnessed electricity, discovered the atom, and taken us to the moon, can actually be our enemy until we learn, by understanding its tricks, how easily it can crucify us.

To place oneself in the present moment is to "remember ourselves," as P. D. Ouspensky calls it, and he points out how we literally lose days and years from our lives by giving them no attention, by moving through time like sleepwalkers, our thoughts wholly absent from what we do. Ouspensky says, "To remember oneself means the same thing as to be aware of oneself—'I am.' Sometimes it comes by itself; it is a very strange feeling. It is not a function, not thinking, not feeling; it is a different state of consciousness. By itself it only comes for very short moments, generally in quite new surroundings, and one says to oneself, 'How strange. I am here.' This is self-remembering; at this moment you remember yourself. . . . Later, when you begin to distinguish these moments, you reach another interesting conclusion . . . that what you remember from childhood are only glimpses of self-remembering."†

He says this, too, paradoxically: "As long as you think about yourself you will not remember yourself."

In his book *The Supreme Identity*, Dr. Hubert Benoit says, "Anguish is . . . an illusion since its causes are illusory. Besides this theoretical demonstration we can obtain a practical demonstration of it: we can prove directly, intuitively, the illusory character of anguish. If in fact at a moment in which I suffer . . . I shift my attention from my thinking to my feeling, if, leaving aside all my mental images, I apply myself to perceiving in myself the famous moral suffering in order to savor it . . . I do not succeed . . . of suffering itself I do not find a scrap. The more I pay attention to the act of feeling, withdrawing thereby my attention from my imaginative film, the less I feel. And I prove then the unreality of my anguish."‡

I can believe this. . . . In one of the most piercingly lonely moments of my life, many thousands of miles from home, nearly exhausted and missing my children, I stood on a balcony in a much more distant country

---

†P. D. Ouspensky, *The Fourth Way* (New York: Alfred A. Knopf, 1957).
‡Hubert Benoit, *The Supreme Identity* (New York: Pantheon Books, 1955).

than Nova Scotia and I looked down into a very lovely garden, seeing none of its beauty, and by a supreme act of will—born of desperation—I succeeded for the fraction of a moment in stopping my turbulent thoughts. And in that moment an incredible calm came over me, so that looking down into that garden I felt I was looking into— But I can't describe what I felt except that it was a moment of intense beauty and peace, as if I looked far below the garden into the depths of something much larger than myself, where something had been waiting for my foolish thoughts to subside so that I could be healed.

It was only a moment; I couldn't hang on to it, I couldn't get it back, but it left a knowledge that there is something inside of us, and accessible to us, if only we can practice reaching it.

During the summer that followed the experience above, I remained unusually tired and my nerves ragged. I had made a difficult trip abroad; during the preceding year I had taught creative writing six mornings a week and had also completed a book, and we had sold a house in Connecticut and moved to a new home in New Jersey. By mid-July I began to lean weakly against walls and cry. One morning I woke up with a strange dream vivid in my mind. In the dream the word "ginsenger" was printed on a piece of paper and below it lay the picture of a root, and I remembered, and could still hear, a voice that added clearly, "pacifier."

The word "ginsenger" was unknown to me. Curious, I looked it up in my dictionary: there was no "ginsenger" but there was the word "ginseng," and in 1971 I'd not heard of ginseng, either. It was described as a Chinese perennial herb (*Panax schinseng*, of the family Araliaceae, the ginseng family) with five-foliate leaves, scarlet berries, and an aromatic root valued locally as medicine. In my son's dictionary there was a picture of a root that matched the picture in my dream, and it said that ginseng had been thought by the Chinese for thousands of years to be an aphrodisiac.

Startled and a little amused, I tucked away the odd little dream but without forgetting it. Six weeks later, during the course of my annual medical checkup, my doctor insisted on a battery of tests, gave me a severe scolding, and told me that my central nervous system was officially, thoroughly, and dangerously tired; he insisted I take tranquilizers for several months.

Not long after this I went to the county library to do some research, and in roaming the aisles a bright new book jacket fairly leaped at me from the stacks: its title was *The Chinese Art of Healing*. Remembering my curious dream in July, I took down the book from the shelf; it was an up-to-date compilation of Chinese medicine written by a research scholar in Switzerland. Ginseng was listed in the index and I turned the pages to find it. Following an analysis of ginseng's medicinal qualities—it contains phosphorus, potassium, calcium, magnesium, sodium, iron, aluminum, silicon, barium, strontium, manganese, titanium, glucose, and volatile oils—the author wrote: "Modern science has found an explanation [for its becoming known as "the herb of eternal life"]: the ginseng root is indeed an important medicinal herb. . . . Although it does not confer eternal life it is, in fact, a first-class regulator of high blood pressure and an excellent means of *tonification for the central nervous system*" (italics mine).*

I do not pretend to understand how a dream in July could prescribe an ancient herb for exactly the condition that a twentieth-century doctor uncovered through tests in September; I can only record it with the usual skepticism of a conditioned mind. But it suggests to me that we have dimensions unawakened in ourselves that science hasn't probed yet, that loneliness may be only a symptom of our adolescence, of our lack of completeness, and that we are never really so alone as we think.

*Stephan Palos, *The Chinese Art of Healing* (St. Louis: Herder & Herder, 1971).

8

People

ONE EVENING AFTER DINNER I
glanced from my kitchen window and
saw a scene fairly typical of my neighborhood, although rarely taking place with such precision. The corner of the village in which I lived
consisted of two occupied houses across the road from
me, and the two lightkeepers' houses on Lighthouse
Road down near the water; at this particular moment
Ida Larkin, the senior lightkeeper's wife, crossed the
road and turned into the Nixons' driveway. From the
rear of the Nixons' house emerged Beryl Crowell, hurrying as usual on her way back to her own house. Over
at Lighthouse Road I saw Isabelle and Ervin, the ju-
nior lightkeeper and his wife, stroll across the highway

to pay a call on the Crowells, and at that moment Audrey Larkin knocked on my door.

Juxtapositions.

This visiting process came as a shock to me. I had moved to East Tumbril expecting uninterrupted time and no distractions, and by December I very nearly packed my bags and fled. In my old life privacy had a value I'd never questioned; it was pursued as if it were the Holy Grail. Only a few years earlier I'd actually had two telephones installed in our house in New Jersey, one of them listed, that I could turn off when I wanted privacy, the other unlisted, so that my children could reach me when the first was turned off. There was an unwritten code in the suburbs that no one stopped in to see a friend without telephoning first to ask if it was convenient; it just wasn't done, it was a heinous social crime. And here I had innocently settled into a village where people arrived on one's doorstep without calling, and sometimes into my kitchen without knocking. It was ironic, it was as if the gods were having sport with me. I sat behind my accumulated barriers with a layer of barbed wire on the fringe for good measure, and the people of East Tumbril simply pushed aside the barbed wire and stepped over the barriers.

Audrey knocks on my door and comes in. She is seventeen when we first meet, and it is she who initiates me into the considerable drama of the village. We sit down at the kitchen table and she tells me about the dance at the community hall on Saturday night, who left with whom, who fought with whom, who said what. Frequently we play a board game called Aggravation, very like Parcheesi but played with marbles. She has made the board herself, painstakingly drilling all the necessary holes in a thick square of plywood, and she makes one for me, too. We play like cutthroats, talking as we shake dice and move marbles across the board. She translates the village for me. . . . I learn that X drinks too much, that R is the best lobsterman in East Tumbril, that L is "mental"—a synonym for poor nerves—that B is getting married soon, and that her curling team won again on Friday night. Audrey plans to be the first member of her family to graduate from high school and she has her mind set on going to college. Her long chestnut hair gleams under the light; she teases me about Americans. "Crazy Americans," she says with a grin.

I had lived in two suburbs, each of these suburbs in the metropolitan area of New York, where people walked into their houses after the stimuli of the day, closed the door, and pulled up the portcullis behind them. Yet at the same time I had come to feel that the ingredients missing in suburban life were concern and warmth. Finding friends was an intricate process, a matter of working down through levels and joining this and joining that; it needed energy, a steady nerve, a compass and a map, and then everything had to be arranged, which aborted any spontaneity because no one wanted to intrude on another's privacy: "I was afraid you might be busy. . . ." An artist friend of mine in Connecticut said about a suburb that she and her husband had just left, "We lived there for a year and when we left I felt we hadn't even creased the sheets."

Bobby drives in. He is "sporting around," as he calls it, for winters are long for him. He is thirty-two, married, with a brand-new first baby. In the summer he works all day at the fire tower back in the woods, alert for signs of forest fires; during droughts he will be there steadily week after week until it rains. He is the only other organic gardener in East Tumbril, a commitment he has come to by instinct and out of a love for natural things. He shows me where to build a bird-feeder out of the wind, using evergreen branches to give the birds shelter. He shows me how to make rabbit snares. We talk about ecology and the deep woods and its wild creatures. I first met him in November when a green Forestry trailer suddenly appeared on the corner of Lighthouse Road and turned out to be a deer-weighing station set up for the month-long hunting season. Bobby was one of the men who split up the shifts, for there was always someone there, night and day. He appeared on my doorstep one morning with an empty jug and asked if he could fill it with water. In return he chopped some wood for me, and I would see him straighten up between ax blows and stare out at the harbor, the clouds, the sky. He hopes one day to farm full-time, as his father did. But in winter he feels the pressure of empty time and sometimes he wants to talk about cities and be told that in cities, too, people can find winters long.

I began to re-examine my feelings about privacy, to wonder if it might not have become a neat and convenient way of shutting out people and involvement. I wondered if by carrying it to an extreme—by making of it a fetish—we might not have lost the infinite variety that would keep us tender.

If privacy is "the quality or state of being apart from company or observation," then in East Tumbril I was obviously under more observation than I'd ever experienced before. During the first November storm it was my neighbor who told me that my barn door had blown out, and if I left my car lights on by accident I was sure to be telephoned within the hour. One day on the beach I slipped on a mound of wet seaweed and kept from falling only by throwing my arms around a huge boulder. The next day Isabelle said she'd heard that I had nearly fallen on the beach: her husband had been watching me from the lighthouse.

Hearing this rather irritated me, yet at the same time I conceded that if I had fallen and broken a leg on the beach, or cracked my skull, I might, without such observation, have waited a good many hours or days for rescue.

It reminded me of Jane Jacobs' book *The Life and Death of American Cities*, in which she describes what happened when urban renewal built superb, monolithic brick-and-glass towers for the city's poor, with elevators, lighted hallways, playgrounds, and privacy for every tenant. What happened were burglaries, rapes, assaults, and hallway muggings. On the other hand, some of the tattiest neighborhoods remained stable and their crime rate low. Where was the difference? It lay in the word "community." The tailor in his shop worked next to his window and kept an observing eye on the neighborhood; the butcher in the meat market knew everyone on the block and took note of any strangers who entered it; people sat on porches and steps and observed what went on around them. Very little could happen without being noted, making it a very poor climate for burglaries or muggings.

It is Nicole who introduces me to the French culture in both East and West Tumbril. She is American but her father was born in the village; at eighteen he left it and emigrated to the United States, where he became an architect. A dozen or more years ago, drawn back to visit a dying relative, he brings Grace and their four children with him and they love East Tumbril, and Paul designs and builds an A-frame summer home down the road from me. Nicole is spending the winter here: to think, write poetry, to convalesce from the hectic sixties when she was deeply involved in the peace movement, and from a marriage born of the sixties that did not survive. She is thirty-one, very beautiful, with long black hair parted in the center, black brows, and gray eyes. It is from her that I learn about the French Mass in the church across the harbor; we go there on Sunday morning and hear a fantastic choir sing madrigals in high, lilting sweet voices, and jambalaya until the foot wants

to tap. We decide to make bayberry candles for
Christmas, and after collecting pounds of the tiny ber-
ries we spend an afternoon boiling and straining, boil-
ing and straining, a gargantuan effort that yields a single
birthday cake-sized candle. Ignobly we add stove wax
to the brew and achieve one corrupted dingy candle for
each of us.

The village had two levels to it, I discovered, composed of the younger and the older generation, each
living by different values. The younger ones were
"Americanized," they knew their television shows, and
those who could afford it owned one or two snowmobiles, and when they built their houses they had picture windows and central heating, either an oil furnace
or electric heat. The younger unmarried men were
often restless; there were drag races on the road at
midnight or a noisy revving of motorcycles, and some
drank heavily at the dances in the hall.

The older inhabitants had preserved the fragrance
of a gentler but leaner age. There had been a time
when fishing had fallen upon troubled times in East
Tumbril, the market for lobsters had collapsed, and
East Tumbril had become a forgotten village. Many of
them had emigrated to the States and had now come
back to live out their lives on pensions or Social Security, like Wilfred, who had played honky-tonk music in
the bars of Boston and brought back with him the
elaborate and marvelous organ with which he could
bring tears to the eyes when he played "Danny Boy."
Some of the older ones had never left, but all of them

shared a memory of harder times that left them content with simplicity. In their homes the source of heat was often a cookstove that occupied the central place in the kitchen and burned oil, or oil and wood. This heat moved into the living room and then drifted upstairs to the bedrooms, which were used only for sleeping. It was this generation, too, that planted gardens, if only potatoes. One felt that if the economy of the entire world collapsed it would make no palpable change in their lives; the affluent years were only a mild surprise in a long succession of government miscalculations. They would continue to chop their own wood, plant their vegetables, bake their own bread.

Grace and Paul have come up for a few days to the A-frame and are giving a party; a "musical evening," Grace calls it, for friends and neighbors. I enter the A-frame tucked away among the trees down near the water, and find a fire glowing in the Franklin stove and chairs and benches pushed back to the walls. Guests begin to filter in and sit down, calling out jokes and greetings to each other. The conversation buzzes—about quilts being made at the New Horizons club, a sick neighbor, the weather. Everyone is waiting for Sifroi.

Sifroi is the fiddler; he walks in shyly with his wife Millie. He is tall, dressed in black, a white shirt, and black string tie: a handsome man with white hair and piercing dark eyes. He takes out his fiddle, tunes it, taps his foot, and begins "Turkey in the Straw."

"You must dance," cries Theotiste, taking me by the

hand. *"Everyone—Nicole, Paul, Grace, Rose—" and young and old we take hands and circle the room. The music grows faster and faster until the circling explodes into an exuberant, improvised square dance and we collapse out of breath and laughing.*

Wilfred arrives, and is persuaded to the piano for some honky-tonk music. We drift to the piano and begin to sing old songs like "When Irish Eyes Are Smiling" and "That Old Gal of Mine." I suddenly realize that only a handful of people in the room are under sixty, and indeed, one woman there is ninety years old. These people have known one another since childhood; they fit together gently, companionably, with an innocence that I'd nearly forgotten existed.

When the party ends, the cars outside are white with frost and the air crisp and clear. I feel bemused, enchanted, as if I have been visiting a dream where time has stood still. I drive home, leave the car in the barn, and walk up the driveway to the lighted house, the stars brilliant overhead. I think of the headlines in the paper today: a new hijacking in Europe, a terrorist's bomb in New York.

I remember something seen on the beach this morning: a sheet of clear transparent ice, like glass, and inside of it, perfectly preserved, a spray of bleached pale grass, each blade etched in white to make an exquisite frozen bouquet. I wonder if it will be there tomorrow.

9

Letting Go

JENINE HAS TELEPHONED THIS MORNing, begging me to come over. I know
something must be terribly wrong because Jenine moves through life trying to bother no
one. Jenine's marriage to Silby has been pulled tortuously out of shape these past months. There is a
young woman in the next village, like a witch dealing
in black magic, who assuages her boredom by casting
spells over husbands other than her own. A year ago
she settled on Silby and turned Jenine into a victim.

When the phone rings I am immersed in writing,
which has been going well for the first time in days. I
am closed in upon myself, so concentrated that the
phone's ring jars me and I answer with the greatest
reluctance. Jenine's voice is naturally melodic and high

but I sense the hysteria behind it. I tell her I will come at once. Not without resentment, however: I look longingly at the work I've been doing and then with a sigh I reach for a sweater and hurry across the fields to her house.

Jenine meets me at the door. "I had to call," she says, tears rising in her eyes. "I can't go on any more like this. I wanted to kill myself a few minutes ago, I knew I would if I didn't call someone."

We sit down and with a cup of coffee between us she pours out her helplessness and her bewilderment. There is a sweetness and a naïveté to Jenine that is very touching. She spent her childhood scrubbing floors, cooking meals, and looking after her brothers and sisters, with almost no time left for homework at night. She and Silby met in high school and married very young. They are thirty-three now, with two children, and their marriage is old: Jenine has no weapons to fight the neighborhood nymph; she can no longer cope with the uncertainty of it and the betrayal.

I go to the telephone and call her doctor, and angrily tell him that tranquilizers are no longer enough, she needs help. I am surprised by my anger, and perhaps he is, too. He will make an appointment with a psychiatrist for her, a marriage counselor some distance away, and will call back.

Some hours later Jenine leaves for her appointment and doesn't come home again: the psychiatrist has advised her to take refuge with a relative while things get sorted out. This brings Silby to my house, and we spend the evening talking and arguing. Before I go to bed there is a call from Jenine, and the next morning I drive ten miles to a village up the coast, searching for her in a maze of small cottages and trailers until I find her.

She tells me, with lifted chin and trembling lips, like a child, "What Silby's been doing isn't *right*."

And then her face changes and she adds with sad wisdom, "I love Silby and I always will, but leaving him like this I feel better. I'm not going back. I'd rather never see him again than have him always going off to *her*."

I am startled by her resolution, awed by this insistence on dignity in her life at any cost. She says she has no self-esteem, but without realizing it she is already struggling toward it, desperately, with almost no tools or defenses.

I drive home thoughtfully. When I enter the house again, the words I'd written on paper twenty-four hours ago are still untouched in my typewriter. I try to remember why they seemed so important. I realize that in East Tumbril I have become accessible, and therefore I am vulnerable: the village pulsates with life and I am being pulled into it. I realize that in coming here I am being drawn into the terrible responsibility of entering its life and living, not just beside my neighbors, but with them. I remember a line from one of Krishnamurti's books: "To be vulnerable is to live, to withdraw is to die."

I look again at the words I'd written on paper. They seem very frail and lifeless. I walk into the kitchen and begin mixing yeast and flour and eggs to make bread, a symbolic impulse to match what I feel rising in me, smooth and soft and very warm.

During my early months in East Tumbril I'd heard about two Americans living on an island not far away. The tales told of them were mystifying and provocative: I was given the impression of a wild-haired, middle-aged couple who seldom came ashore—perhaps only at the full of the moon?—and walked hand in hand between store and post office. Her name was Ellen; his was Joe. They had bought the island, moved in, and were attempting to become self-sufficient. She had been a doctor, he a building contractor, but on the island he'd built a house raised on beams—shocking —with no basement under it. There was a windmill, or there would be. Hearing about them—it all sounded interesting—I expressed a vague interest in meeting them.

One evening in early March the telephone rang and a strange voice said that if I wanted to go to the island the next morning I would be picked up by two people named Brad and Lucy, who would be delivering mail and a buzz saw to the islanders. I said, "Fine," and "What time?" and then I hung up and was gripped by the urgent need—very urgent—to say no.

I realized that I had just agreed to deliver myself into the hands of two complete strangers for my first trip on a lobster boat to an island I'd never seen where I would meet two more strangers. I didn't even know who had called me. Such was my history that whenever I'd left home for a few hours or a day I had left children behind, there had been arrangements to make: directions about meals, a telephone number where I could be reached in case of crisis, all managed under the assumption that it was done for the sake of my children. Now I began to wonder if it wasn't myself that had needed reassuring. I could leave a note behind me this time but who would read it? Who would know I'd gone? For that matter, who would even know if I returned or not?

I pictured myself carried off to a remote island and abandoned there with a few tins of food—I hoped to God someone remembered a can opener. I pictured the ransom note already written—*send money or she will die*—and I tried to remember how much money Christopher and Jonathan had in their accounts: would my abductors settle for two hundred dollars in nickels and dimes? I couldn't think of anyone who would be willing to pay a ransom and I could see the scorn on the faces of my abductors when they realized no one found me worth saving. It would turn into one of those Hollywood farces where no one knew what to do with me. . . . Or perhaps Brad and Lucy would turn out to be reliable but it was their *boat* that would prove unreliable. It would sink without warning, leaving no traces behind, and weeks, months from now my children would walk into an empty house and say, "Where could she have gone? Where can she be?" There would be unwashed breakfast dishes in the sink— there always were—a book open on the couch, a jacket missing . . .

The whole thing felt like the supreme existential experience, an act of faith, a plunge over the precipice into the unknown, a letting go of every carefully contrived illusion by which I assured myself that I was secure, immortal, and vital.

Brad and Lucy arrived on my doorstep at ten o'clock the next morning, looking disheveled but certainly not sinister in their fishing boots, sweaters, jackets, and caps: Brad was lean and slouching, his wife stolid and hearty. I was whisked off in their truck to the wharf and handed down into Brad's boat. Ropes were cast off, the engine purred, and suddenly I was on the water instead of looking at it from the shore, I was standing on the deck of a boat with sea spray and sun on my face, and for the first time I was seeing the other side of the lighthouse, and my own house sitting tamely on its hill. We moved out of the harbor, going against the wind, detoured to hail a passing lobster boat, stopped to check a neighbor's mackerel seine, and after an hour on the water the boat pulled into the leeward side of the island.

It was a long island, three miles in length and wooded. On this south side I could see barbed-wire fencing, a primitive dirt road that vanished among the trees, and the roofs of three buildings. A tractor appeared and slowly maneuvered its way down the road to the shore. A dory was shoved into the water and Joe began rowing out to us.

I had to smile as the dory drew closer. Joe was a lithe, slender man with a white beard—a sight we are quite accustomed to in America—and with no signs of vampirism at all. He even hailed us warmly. In a few minutes I was being rowed in the dory to the shore and before he turned to go back and bring in the buzz saw he pointed the way to the house. "The goats are off somewhere else, so it won't be an obstacle race for you," he said. "Ellen's making head cheese. Just follow the road, you'll find her."

I walked through a series of primitive gates and then through a sea of mud. I passed a storage house, a shed-roofed barn, and nodded to a number of piglets lying in the sun. Beyond lay the largest building, built of vertical boards, with a long line of windows facing south. It was very quiet except for the grunts from the piglets. It all vaguely resembled a summer camp in the woods, not yet opened for the season. I climbed a rough wooden ladder to a porch, knocked on the screened door, heard a voice inside, and walked in.

Ellen was unexpected, too: a fragile, slender woman with long white hair worn in a single braid that fell over one shoulder to her waist. And she *was* making head cheese, which came from the first pig they'd slaughtered, and she *was* a doctor. And still one, she assured me humorously, having been up half the night with a sick goat.

The structure in which they lived was composed of one large room and one small. The larger room was piled high in the center with boxes not yet unpacked; there was nowhere to put things until cupboards could be built and they were too busy to manage such luxurious extras yet. There was a generator, which they ran for a few hours in the evening, for light. The refrigerator operated on bottled gas. Their heat came from an assortment of wood stoves placed in various corners in the living room. Even so, they had areas already outlined: a couch in one corner, a dining table in another, a work-and-sewing area in another, a line of bait barrels along the south wall in which they were raising cabbage, lettuce, cherry tomatoes, and herbs.

But mostly they lived now in the lean-to kitchen, centering their lives on the wood-burning cookstove which magnificently heated this smaller space. The walls were of rough board; outside lay the latrine. It was a strange place to find a doctor.

"I love it," she said. "I was fed up with running around in circles, and Joe was fed up in his own way, too. We met and decided to pool our talents and try it. Like that," she said, snapping her fingers.

They had arrived on their island only a few months before I had come to East Tumbril, and the logistics behind their getting there at all were incredible. Everything had to be carried out by boat; it would be another year before they could begin clearing enough land to raise their own feed for the livestock, and in the meantime hay had to be brought from the mainland. At the moment Ellen was cooking pounds of Irish moss and fish each day for the pigs to eat.

Joe took me on a tour of the barn: hens roosting on every beam, dozens of rabbits in hutches along the walls, a milking platform for the goats, the new piglets and the sows. We lingered over the lunch they'd prepared for us. It was a very sumptuous lunch: Ellen confessed that she spent most of the day in the kitchen trying out new gourmet dishes.

"As well as drying, canning, salting, and preserving," pointed out Joe, drawing on his pipe.

"Which," said Ellen, smiling, "I never had a chance to do before. I was always too busy."

They were busy here, too. They worked, literally, from dawn to dusk, feeding the animals, learning animal husbandry, chopping wood, clearing lands for gardens, constantly renewing fences that the goats butted down, and working toward their goal of becoming completely self-sufficient.

"I figure two more years," said Ellen.

"Three," said Joe, shaking his head. "Don't forget the sauna we're going to build."

After lunch Joe and Brad went down to the beach to finish setting up the buzz saw and test it out, and Ellen, Lucy, and I wandered along the beach talking, collecting shells, and getting acquainted. Ellen was showing me their garden down near the water— mounds of seaweed in which they hoped to raise a year's supply of potatoes for the pigs—when I suddenly looked up and saw the head and shoulders of a goat silhouetted against the sky. Ellen, following my gaze, said, "That's William." A moment later another head appeared, and then another, and suddenly we were surrounded by Nubian goats, nuzzling and nudging and pushing and shoving, and Ellen was introducing each one by name.

"Give me an island and a mug-up," said Brad when he pulled anchor, "and I'd be the happiest man in the world." He said this gazing wistfully back at the shore, where Ellen and Joe stood waving at us. I knew how he felt because I felt that way, too: a little enchanted, dreamy, and very peaceful. An island, I realized, was a very special place: all the way back to East Tumbril the boat plowed up and down through choppy seas and I scarcely noticed.

But it wasn't entirely the island, of course, or the making of four new friends, either. Something was different in me. Some final mysterious umbilical cord— to earth and to all things trivial—had been cut. I had become rearranged, and the pattern was looser.

$$10$$

Arrivals and Departures / Change

 I WENT BACK TO NEW JERSEY THAT first Christmas; the lease on the apartment wouldn't expire for several more months and Christopher was living there while he commuted to classes in New York. It seemed easier for me to leave Nova Scotia than for both sons to come to East Tumbril. No, I'll take that back: I didn't want to force my new lifestyle on them too early, and for this holiday season. I wasn't sure yet what they would *do* with East Tumbril.

I arrived exhilarated by the crowds, lights, and noises, and an hour later Jonathan arrived, too. Christopher has pointed out that we always talk feverishly on the first and last evenings that we're together, and between these two points of reference go our separate ways. And this is true: tomorrow Kit will be closeted in his room working over a poem, and Jonathan will be off seeing his old friends from high school, and I, since I arrived, have been politely ignoring the piles of dirty clothes I see in their bedroom, the grease in the kitchen sink and in artistic spatter patterns on the counter: that is what *I* will be doing tomorrow. But this is First Evening and Kit is on his feet imitating someone he's recently met—he's a wonderful mimic—and Jonathan is laughing as he brings out Cokes from the refrigerator: his turn will come next. Jonathan has said, after visiting other families, that we are the only family he's met that doesn't spend the first few hours of a vacation discussing who will get the car, and when, and for what. I am always startled by these appraisals, and secretly cherish them. I have filed this away with the picture Kit drew of me when he was in kindergarten. Every child had to draw an impression of his or her mother, and struggling toward some Gesell-and-Spock élan that seemed forever out of reach, I was touched by the perfectly normal and smiling stick figure he drew. It is my deficiency that I never know what other families talk about when they meet, or how my children see me.

I collapse happily into bed at two in the morning, and as I listen to the sounds of traffic outside I remember that this day began in East Tumbril with the sound of wind and surf. I cannot make this real: East Tumbril suddenly has the remoteness of a dream that I dreamed the night before.

*   *   *

The next morning, even before breakfast, I begin telephoning my friend Betsy, of whom I am very fond but who never writes letters. I begin early because she turns off her telephone when she's busy and has to be caught during lulls. Even so it's evening before I reach her.

"You're here!" she shouts. "How long will you be staying?"

"Two weeks," I tell her. "How about lunch soon?"

"I can't wait to see you. Lunch," she murmurs. "Lunch. Damn, one of the children must have moved my appointment book."

I say in awe, "Betsy, you have an appointment book now?"

"Oh, God yes, I have to, it's the only way." She names church and political committees, her own classes, her children's classes, indoor tennis once a week, and imposed on this the usual holiday parties and distractions. "Wait 'til I find . . . here it is."

She goes through her appointment book day by day; she goes through it three times. The only day that she is free for lunch is the day before I'm to leave. We each write down the date solemnly. I feel as if I'm making an appointment with my dentist, she even says before we ring off, "Look, if any time opens up before then I'll call you, there's just the slightest chance that next Tuesday. . ."

I'd forgotten how busy life is in the suburbs.

I begin Christmas shopping, a real treat after ordering nearly everything in East Tumbril from a Simpson-

Sears or Eaton's catalogue and waiting a month for delivery. My list is long and I find myself walking through the shops in a state of perpetual wonder at the abundance, at the glittering, clever, and ingenious possibilities. I marvel and walk home with arms full of packages.

But on my second foray something strange happens: I find myself standing on the first floor of the department store with purses to the south of me, men's silk shirts to the east, a long line of pastel cosmetics and fragrances to the west, the gloves-scarfs-and-umbrellas counter to the north, and suddenly, unbidden, there comes a sense of unease, of glut. There is too much; I feel overwhelmed, almost stifled after the leanness of the past months. I have grown accustomed to essentials and my glance finds nothing essential here, nothing that hasn't been polished, decorated, fantasized, satirized, satinized, inflated. I feel a sense of revulsion; I turn and flee.

I go to a dinner party with Janet and Rod Putnam. I've known Janet and Rod for ten years, and so they are now very old friends, considering the way life is these days. Our host and hostess have a new home, and we become absorbed in seeing it and admiring it, and in catching up on news of mutual friends. Over coffee the host turns to me and says, "It's high time you told us about your move to Nova Scotia, which I certainly envy your doing."

"Yes," his wife says, "I'm so curious. Tell us, for instance, what you do every day."

I am about to reply when Janet intervenes. She says quickly, crisply, and dismissingly, "Oh, I can tell you that. She gets up at dawn, chops wood, milks the cows, builds fires, does a little writing, eats fish, and goes to bed at sunset. Now tell me," she continues, "what you've heard about the Johnsons' divorce."

I have known Janet, as I say, for ten years: has she always been so brittle?

There is a meeting—a meeting in the truest sense —that comes, oddly, at the electrical supply house. I have determined to replace something called an electrical ceiling strip that had been lost in moving; it has been impossible to find one in Nova Scotia and it is high on my list of things to take back.

The man who waits on me spends a long time searching, and when he unearths the last one in the shop he is as pleased as I. I ask him to explain it to me in case the electrician who will install it runs into any problems.

"If he does, just tell him to call us," he says.

I explain that it isn't that simple, I live in Nova Scotia now.

"Nova Scotia!" he said, his face brightening. "The wife and I are certainly interested in Nova Scotia. What's it like to actually live there? Are people friendly?"

"Very," I tell him, and explain my plans. "Do you garden?"

"As much as I can," he says. "How much land do you have? I'm retiring in two years and the wife and

I've been talking about either Wisconsin or Nova Scotia. We don't like it here any more, it's changed. People have stopped caring, they're too busy. But damned if I know what they're so busy doing, either."

"Why is it, do you think?"

"Lemmings rushing to the sea," he says scornfully.

"It must be in the air," I tell him, "because I've been here only two days and I've begun rushing, too. I can't seem to help it."

We talk about raising vegetables, and the land, and being in touch again with what matters, and why it matters, and then a new customer comes in. We shake hands and he wishes me the best of luck and I wish him the same. "I've enjoyed this," he says, and we part warmly, having exchanged the best of ourselves, our dreams.

Life moves very fast these days, with accelerating change, and paradoxically we move faster and faster within it in search of permanence. We are jealous of what change does to us and angry at its constancy, which I suspect is due to the knowledge buried inside of us that one day there will come a final change that slides us off the face of the earth. But we're not at all consistent: we castigate change when it *removes* something or someone from our lives, and we call this loss, but when change *adds* something to our lives we assume this was only our due and forget that this, too, is change. Life is always impartial, and in motion. Every relationship in our lives has to grow or to die; only for a few moments can it be held in a state of suspension before it begins a slow, inexorable movement toward growth or toward decay. Even a memory is no more alive than a butterfly pinned to a board. When we live with a memory we live with a corpse; the impact of the experience has changed us once but can never change us again.

We have no choice but to accept the subtractions and multiplications of change. Every day and every hour we lose a portion of our life to the tick of the clock. We lose parents, wives, husbands, marriages, friends, children, illusions, but there is this to be added: nothing ever ends without something new beginning. This, too, is a law of life.

Emerson writes in his beautiful essay "Compensation," "The death of a dear friend, wife, brother, lover, which seems nothing but privation, somewhat later assumes the aspect of a guide or genius; for it commonly operates revolutions in our way of life, terminates an epoch of infancy or of youth which was waiting to be closed, breaks up a wonted occupation or household or a style of living, and allows the formation of new ones more friendly to the growth of character.

"And the man or woman," he concludes, "who would have remained a sunny garden-flower with no room for its roots and too much sunshine for its head, by the falling of the walls and the neglect of the gardener is made the banyan of the forest, yielding shade and fruit to wide neighborhoods of men."

The fact of the matter is that without change we would have to choose one day or one hour in our lives, like Emily in *Our Town*, and remain fixed there, going round and round in a circle, incapable of stepping out, incapable of motion or growing because even a new thought would change us. Sometimes that is how people live anyway, those who cannot tolerate change, and so they die. Not physically but inside; there are more walking dead among us than we know.

Nor can we hurry change, which has a calendar of its own. The best and the unique turnings in life are never forced, their roots have been growing in us underground for a long time, without our conscious notice, awaiting only what Jung calls a "meaningful coincidence," a chance encounter, a phrase that haunts the ear, a meeting, an invitation, an insight or revelation. All life asks of us is that we stay open to clues. Nothing forced or done in a frenzy works in our truest interests. If we look back on paths taken and not taken we can, with the wisdom of hindsight, see that something works inside us like yeast, if only we pay attention, and it is always toward growth if we obey it.

I once thought my own life was changeless and that already I'd been embalmed; I was stuck—helpless—and I wrote in my journal one day, "Will nothing ever change, will it be like this forever?" and I wrote that word "forever" all the way down the page, over and over, in my frustration and despair. I even considered ending my life and went so far as to root out a pistol from an old trunk in the attic, but then I thought, "I'll give it a few months; if I can just get through the next hour perhaps I can manage a day, and if I can manage a day I'll cross it out with an X on the calendar, and somehow a week may pass." After ten days I forgot to cross off the days with an X, and a few months later I was alive again, and full of hope. Life, always in motion, had gone on changing events and circumstances, as well as me. The currents that had brought me to that moment also carried me beyond it. Life never stands still. If I had known this I might have had more faith.

But it was never death I faced that day anyway, it was life. And change. And growing.

The Chinese, three thousand years ago, created a Book of Changes, the *I Ching*, perhaps the first human effort to record both the outer and the inner universe. Frequently it's used as a book of divination but its wisdom has fed both Confucianism and Taoism, and just to scan its pages is to glimpse the motion of life: obstruction followed by deliverance, agitation by peace, going away by returning. Jung calls life "a flux, a flowing into the future." Saint-Exupéry says, "Life is sustained by movement, not by a foundation."

The Christmas tree was divested of lights and the decorations packed away for another year. Christopher's classes resumed and Jonathan packed his suitcase; I did more laundries and made my own travel reservations. For two weeks I had not been able to make my life in East Tumbril seem real but there had begun to grow in me a strange hunger.

When the plane landed in Nova Scotia the earth was still brown and the sun shining; we had outraced the snow that was falling in Boston when we left. I rescued the car from the parking lot and began the drive to East Tumbril, my eyes already beginning the adjustment to space and sky and water. At the general store I stopped for bread and milk and Emil gave me his broad, kind smile. "So you're back," he said. "Have a nice trip?"

"Fine," I said. "Have a good Christmas?"

I drove on to the house, parked the car, and unlocked the door. I carried in my typewriter, changed into jeans and boots, and headed at once for the beach. A steady northwest wind had turned the sunny harbor a dark and angry blue trimmed with white ruffles and lace. The air was tangy with salt and cold.

I climbed to the top of a high flat rock and shouted at the top of my voice, "Friends, Romans, countrymen..."

A sea gull flew away, startled, and the wind scattered my words. I laughed and climbed down and went up the hill to unpack; it was time to get the hurry out of my life and the deadly efficiency I'd grown like new skin. Yesterday at this hour I'd been delivering Jonathan to his train, and in the morning there had been a trip to the bank, a visit to the grocery store, and then —oh yes, that hurried lunch with Betsy, very hurried because suddenly it was *I* who was running out of time. And now it was *that* world that was unreal.

Arrivals and departures... losses and gains. We can never balance the accounts of our life. The only abiding sense of permanence—of centeredness and stability—has to come from inside of us. We are like small boats moving toward the ocean, sometimes in convoy and sometimes alone; the scenery and the cast of characters keep changing. Nothing, as Emerson points out, can bring us peace but ourselves.

11

Men and Women —

 SEVEN OR EIGHT YEARS AGO I WAS talking to a doctor whom I knew. We had lately moved to a new town and he had been very kind in giving counsel on getting acquainted with and adjusted to this suburb. We had been talking and suddenly he said, looking at me over steepled fingers as if I were a problem to be solved, "You know, you'd make someone a great wife. Have you thought of marrying again?"

I told him that I felt a good marriage was probably the most creative and satisfying thing that a person could accomplish in a lifetime but that I simply hadn't met a man who tempted me.

He said, nodding wisely, "It's your children."

Startled, I said, "My what?"

"It puts men off. They'd have to support your children and send them to college and that's enough to frighten away the best of men."

Astonished, I said, "Good heavens, I happen to support my two children very nicely, thank you." And I told him what my income had been the previous year.

It was his turn to be astonished. He said accusingly, "You don't *look* as if you made that much money."

I replied indignantly, "I wouldn't *want* a man who measures me by the clothes I wear and the income I look as if I have."

To which he replied tartly, "And he wouldn't want you either."

That was the end of the exchange but it's returned to me a number of times since then, with all its ramifications, which, unless I misunderstood, seem considerable. He was suggesting that to be "neat but not gaudy" was not enough: I needed packaging. Instead of living in a comfortable, sunny little house I should, presumably, if I wanted to marry, live in a large house with a large mortgage and never step out of that house unless I looked as if I were stepping out of the pages of a fashion magazine. A man would then understand that I was worth knowing and having.

The doctor may be right, I don't know, it all depends on what you want. All I know is that I can't measure people by their incomes or their possessions, and the people who measure themselves by these values have no appeal at all for me. Which makes it a standoff. But then my particular problem has been that when I see "Before" and "After" photographs on the beauty pages of a magazine I usually prefer the "Before" photos. It's a flaw in me.

In East Tumbril when Frank came to plow a third garden for me he lingered for a few minutes to chat and asked me if I didn't mind living by myself. After a moment's reflection on my reply he announced with a grin that I must hate men to be contented living alone. This was at least direct; Frank doesn't feel it's because I've not been repackaged.

One day men and women are going to stop facing each other across a chasm of doubt and suspicion and learn how to be friends, which is what the best of marriages are based on, anyway. I have been married, but it turned out that we had never become friends and so when everything fell apart there was no frame of reference on which to rebuild. Friends ask me curiously what it is I look for now, assuming I want too much, or have become too hard to please. I tell them "tenderness" and "friendship." A man could be four feet tall and not have a sou to his name but if he is capable of friendship with a woman I would follow him to the ends of the earth. Friendship implies shared understanding, shared humor, a certain openness and honesty. Sometimes we ask for much less when we marry.

I know such friendships must be possible because I grew up with boys; in fact, I didn't find a girl companion until I was ten years old, but I was as close to one of those boys as I was to anyone else, or have been since. When we were ten, eleven, twelve, and thirteen he and I shared rebellions, confidences, hopes, dreams, fears, and complete equality; it was good, so that I know friendship between girls and boys is possible. Between men and women I don't know.

The boy to whom I was closest as a child was tragically killed while he was still young, and so I can't measure what happened to him as he grew up, or whether he could sustain such a friendship now. I have, however, met one of the boys I knew less well when I was growing up; in fact, I encountered him not long ago at the only school reunion I've attended. With Arthur I had roller-skated, organized a gang, fought snowball fights, and enjoyed more than a few spin-the-bottle kisses. I first saw him as he crossed the floor of the auditorium and as he passed the table at which I sat I jumped up and called out, "Arthur! For heaven's sake, Arthur Bayberry!"

He turned and looked at me.

Under that chilling gaze I heard myself say weakly, "It's Dorothy, remember? The Handy Street snowball gang, and we used to race on roller skates—"

He lifted one eyebrow and drawled, "My God, I hope you never tell anyone that." Carrying his adult image intact, and without so much as a handshake, he walked out of my life again, and that was that.

I sat down and said, "Good Lord, what's happened to Arthur?"

"Arthur's a corporation executive now," said my companion, "and for starters he's been married four times and divorced four times."

Obviously something had happened to Arthur on the way to adulthood and he was sealed up tight now, brittle, no longer vulnerable, and safe. Life had produced another casualty. Arthur, I suspected, would continue to replace wives like washing machines and grow more and more cynical about love.

Women are casualties, too. Especially women. I have met widowed and divorced women—young ones, too—who cling to expensive, unmanageable homes because without the status of that house they feel they would have no identity at all; it doesn't occur to them to go out and search for that identity. I meet women who sit and wait for improbable rescues—tomorrow, next month, or next year; it hasn't occurred to them to rescue themselves. "How can women learn to survive—and learn to value survival?" asks Phyllis Chesler in her book *Women and Madness*. "How can women banish self-sacrifice, guilt, naïveté, helplessness, madness and sorrow from the female condition?. . . . Women must somehow free themselves to be concerned with many things, and ideas, and with many people."*

Yes, I'm a feminist. I *like* women. But we've been male-oriented for so long that we've come to believe we don't matter unless a man gives us significance. The waste of it makes me angry. I think that being single—widowed, divorced, never married, and of either sex—should carry with it the special obligation—even the responsibility—to live a little differently, with some élan, certainly with as much spirit as possible and with a sense of adventure denied the more domesticated. There are so many things that married people can't do.

*Phyllis Chesler, *Women and Madness* (Garden City, N.Y.: Doubleday & Company, 1972).

It's true that it's a world of couples, and always will be, but married people often live quite circumscribed lives, and frequently very monotonous lives.

It's simply that I hate waste. If I had to define evil, or sin, or wickedness I would point to waste: waste of talent, waste of potential, waste of freedom, women, men, food, and the earth's resources as well. This includes prisons, poverty, alienation, bad education, pollution, and what happens to people when they prefer shadows to sunlight.

Not long ago I received a letter from a woman I've known since my school days. I'd lost touch with her lately, and frankly I confess I'd not tried very hard to stay in touch because since the death of her husband her letters had become dreary exercises in self-pity. This was particularly irritating because she is a talented woman but also because her husband had been extremely difficult to live with: a petty tyrant and an alcoholic as well. Following his death, Sybil chose to withdraw from life and to lift her dead husband to sainthood. I had wanted to shake her and say, "Hey— start living!"

Sybil's current letter is ecstatic and filled with radiance. Sybil is having a peak experience now: there is passion in every line, her letter quivers with feeling, she has become a crusader for life, she is soaring. But what has accomplished this is that she is writing from a hospital bed where she has learned that she has an incurable illness.

Sybil has been *shocked* into awareness.

Answering her letter is going to be very hard. It's a

beautiful letter and, faced with her exultation, I want
to genuflect in front of it, but it is going to be difficult
to congratulate Sybil when that sense of significance,
of now-ness and realization, has been available to her
all along.

It's the waste of it that matters.

For half my life I've nursed a cockeyed vision of
Judgment Day in which we all give testimony to what
we've done with our lives and with those one or two or
three talents that God has given us according to the
biblical parable. In this confrontation God asks the big
question, and we say, "Well, God, I was awfully busy
doing such and such for my children—there were a
great many sacrifices to make for them, you know—
and then I did thus and so for my husband, and then
by that time—"

And He says patiently (for in the sight of God one
assumes there is no difference between men and
women), "Very good, my dear, but when I gave you
those talents you had neither husband nor children—
they were yours entirely by choice—and therefore
quite unconnected with the question, which is . . . What
did you do with those talents—the brain I gave to you
as well as the heart, the capacity for joy, the integrity
and the curiosity, the uniqueness that I gave to you
personally, to develop and multiply as an individual?"

I feel that it was good for my children as well as for
me to live in East Tumbril. My older son is at heart a
traditionalist, and only an ancestral family home would
have suited him, but I had taken a long look at that
possibility and not liked what I saw: a waiting Pene-

lope keeping warm the hearth fires in an outgrown milieu and thinking backward instead of forward. It had been just the three of us for so long, and I had always been available. I think that we have become the better acquainted for the space around us now. Jonathan sees this more clearly, perhaps, but then he is majoring in psychology and is currently doing research into sexual stereotypes among men and women. His generation may not know the answers yet but they've begun to ask the questions.

12

The Unseen / Speculations

ONE WINTRY AFTERNOON, GLANCING
out of my window, I saw a family of
pheasant emerge from the hill below the
house to scout for food in the grass. They walked as
far as the path, quite boldly, their long slender throats
forming the most graceful S I've ever seen. During another winter I had an uninvited tenant, a squirrel or
rat, in the wall of my kitchen; without ever meeting we
grew to know each other quite well. When I sat down
to dinner I would hear him enter near the kitchen
door, make his way up the wall, and cross the ceiling
to settle down over my head. If he took too long to
arrange himself I would climb on my chair and thump,
telling him he could share the house only if he was
quiet. After I thumped I wouldn't hear him again until

the next evening at dinnertime. He kept hours even more regular than mine.

Animals and insects have their own form of consciousness and more of it, I think, than we may realize. When my comfrey plants bloomed they attracted swarms of bees, dozens to each huge plant, and coming late to harvest I would have to join them. I began by telling them very frankly that I meant no harm. Sometimes we would meet over the same leaf but they were always content to share and no bee ever stung me. One evening I picked blueberries along the path below the house and heard a bird singing and chirping nearby: I spotted him twelve feet away on the slim branch of an alder. When I moved down the path to a new berry patch he followed and continued singing from the branch of another alder, again twelve feet away. And so it went, all the way down the path to the beach. I only wished I could translate what he was saying, and if you feel that I'm suggesting the bees and the bird "knew" me, I would say, Why not? There are other languages than the spoken word.

I collect the invisible, it fascinates me. The nice thing about extrasensory perception, for instance—your common, well-documented garden variety of ESP—is that it proves we don't know everything yet, and possibly very little at all, which is healthier than arrogance. We have very limited perception: our responses may be as delayed as the ray of light that takes sixteen minutes to reach us from the sun. Being attuned to what we can touch, taste, smell, and see, we overlook how much in our lives is invisible: love, for instance; thought, God, the future, time, faith, hope, and even the electricity that brings us light.

We ourselves are essentially invisible—the part of us that matters to other people—because no one can see our thoughts or read our feelings. We're like icebergs, only the surface showing, and the rest concealed but very alive and powerful. I tell you what I want to tell you, depending on my honesty and openness. In replying you select from a wealth of possibilities inside you, censoring and rearranging, and if the truth remains unspoken there is no way I can probe deeper without your consent. There are some people who are like tightly capped wine bottles, completely inaccessible; they refuse to give away anything they think or feel, and if you know them over a long period of time —reluctantly, of course—you still don't know them, they are like one-dimensional paper dolls. If you should have to spend a few hours with them they are the people who "rob you of your solitude without providing companionship."

Maurice Nicoll writes, "It is impossible for me to say that I know anybody and it is equally impossible to say that anybody knows me. For while I see all your bodily movements and outward appearances . . . yet I cannot see *in* you and do not know what you are, and can never know . . . only you have this direct access. I and everyone else can see and hear you. The whole world might see and hear you. But only you can know yourself."*

*Maurice Nicoll, *Living Time* (London: Vincent Stuart, 1952).

The other day I was reading an article in the *New York Times* about kidney transplants among members of the same family. The motivations of the donor and of the recipient were discussed and were, it seemed, a matter of more than casual importance. A doctor was quoted as saying that a kidney transplant is most likely to succeed if "the fantasies of donor and recipient coincide." He mentioned a case where a sister only grudgingly agreed to contribute a kidney and he said, "The transplant between the two sisters might have worked if both had believed the operation would reconcile them." Because of the angry emotions they shared, however, the doctor predicted—and quite correctly—that the transplanted kidney would not function long.†

One would think that, once blood types have been matched, a kidney is a kidney. What strange alchemy of hatred or resentment is transmitted, invisible to the microscope, along with the organ?

I was talking once to a psychiatrist about someone for whom I felt deeply sorry. "Yes," he said, nodding, "that is very interesting, don't you think? He makes even me feel sorry for him."

Something in his voice caused me to look closely at him. "What do you mean?"

"I mean that he feels very sorry for himself, does he not? He would like you to feel sorry for him, too. One picks it up out of the air."

At that time such an idea was new to me, a revelation, but I've tested it out many times, and it's true. I

†*New York Times*, about July 15, 1977.

once had a neighbor who was vivacious and charming and yet each time we parted I went home reeling, my world darkened and my optimism in shreds. I realized at last that from behind the charming mask she was sending out death rays with the efficiency of a "Star Trek" phaser gun. The last time I saw her she complained that people never returned to see her. I could have told her why: the cost was too high, the period of convalescence too long.

Now I notice how a person affects me, and no longer call it coincidence, for whether we realize it or not we are all of us transmitting stations, sending out and receiving signals invisible to the naked eye and at too high a frequency for the ear to consciously hear. But something in us knows.

This something—the unconscious or the subconscious—may prove to be the rudder and sail of our lives, guiding and instructing us out of a knowledge that jumps across all our time concepts. Precognition is inexplicable by every law of existing logic, and yet it happens. If I doubt this I need only go back to a short story that I wrote in the fifties, a decade before that seemingly placid life fell apart with the suddenness of Longfellow's *One Hoss Shay*. At the time that I wrote the short story I was one half of the Perfect Couple, immersed in the Ideal Marriage, and if someone had shown me the future no one would have been more shocked than I. In this story an old woman named Sate Timball lies dying in a Berkshire town. In looking back on her life she describes a marriage that ended when she was forty, and a curious encounter that followed the ending of that marriage; it is the encounter that is the focus of the story. In four sentences she dissects that marriage, with an insight and knowledge unknown to me at that time, using words that I would hear repeated almost verbatim to me by a psychiatrist some ten years later, when I was forty. The encounter that is the heart of the story happened to me as well. It is as if, in writing the story, I was looking back on my own life from a point of time that had not occurred yet ... as if something in me already knew.

Spirit, too, is invisible, an intangible in our lives. Epictetus says that we are "small souls bearing up corpses," a rather lugubrious suggestion but true in a sense. Perhaps we could change that to "physical shells activated by spirit" or hollow vessels filled or half filled with livingness. In his book *The Transparent Self*, Dr. Sidney Jourard describes all the latent diseases and viruses that occupy our bodies at any given moment of our lives, and he writes that the real question is not "Why do people get sick?" but rather "Why aren't people sick all the time?" He believes that we become ill when we grow *dispirited*. When we're *inspirited*—happy, confident, creative—the same viruses that live in us find us impervious to attack.

He sets up an imaginary scale on which to measure spirit, or "spirit-titre," as he calls it. "If," he suggests, "spirit-titre can be measured on a scale of from one to one hundred, with a normal reading in the range of from thirty to sixty," then at a "forty-five level, modal behavior is possible but the body-system is not overly resistant to the ubiquitous germs, viruses, or effects of stress that are the inexorable consequences of the very way of life called 'respectability.'"

Ah, respectability!

When, however, the "spirit-titre falls below some wellness-sustaining level—say, around 20 or 30 units —the person is characterized subjectively by low spirits, depression, boredom, diffuse anxiety. . . . Doubtless, in time, the low spirit-titre permits 'illness' to take root: microbes or viruses multiply, stress by-products proliferate, latent illnesses become manifest or galloping."

He suggests that the majority of illnesses are really the means by which a dispirited person is saying, "Help, I can't cope any more," and that, given someone to listen, even a placebo would heal him.

"If it be true," he writes, "as some psychoanalysts maintain, that God is a symbol of man's never-reached ultimate powers, and that man has denied or become alienated from his powers, then if prayer and worship are effective in helping a man re-own these powers, we ought to learn more about prayer. If man's powers of healing are rooted in his own body, but man doesn't know this . . . and believes instead that the power of healing is 'out there,' in the physician's black bag, then displaying the black bag perhaps is *not* the most effective way of mobilizing man's self-healing power, or spirit. I think that once we begin to seriously study 'spirit' as a natural phenomenon, we will not only increase our grasp of nature's laws but we will radically alter many of our practical pursuits."‡

Nature's laws... A "new" mystery surfaces, such as acupuncture or faith healing, and we marvel, and then the "experts" begin to systematically knock it down, saying that it cannot work because it shouldn't. But by what laws is it illogical if it works? In his book *Medicine Power*, Brad Steiger quotes a one-hundred-year-old medicine man named Thomas Largewhiskers as saying, "I don't know what you learned from books but the most important thing I learned from my grandfathers was that there is a part of the mind that we don't really know about and that it is that part that is most important in whether we become sick or remain well."*

In continuing to collect the invisible I have lately ordered a pyramid: a large one to meditate under and a number of tiny ones under which I will experiment with drying foods. The rationalist may be appalled at this, but strange things are happening under pyramids, so long as they remain in scale to the pyramid of Cheops: apples remain fresh and juicy, milk doesn't sour for a surprising length of time. Why this is so, no one knows. It teases the mind—both mine and the scientists struggling to explain it; one more hint that we live in a world where the invisible has more portent

‡Sidney M. Jourard, *The Transparent Self* (Princeton, N.J.: D. Van Nostrand & Co., 1964).
*Brad Steiger, *Medicine Power* (Garden City, N.Y.: Doubleday & Company, 1974).

than anything we may see with our 20–20 vision. Did
the ancient Egyptians, perhaps, know secrets of the
universe we are blind to? Were they a more advanced
people than we?

As archaeologists continue to dig up new civilizations and to expand the time of man on this earth, we
may discover that we are only a small hiccup among
vaster civilizations. Ouspensky points out that "the
usual view of text-books and popular 'outlines of history' which contain a very short historical period and a
more or less dark age before that, is in reality very far
from the most recent scientific views ... the 'stone age'
is regarded with more probability as a period not of
the beginning but of the fall and degeneration of *pre-
viously existing civilizations* [italics mine]. ... All savage or semi-savage peoples have tales and traditions of
a golden age ... All people had—*before*—better
weapons, better boats, better towns, higher forms of
religion. The same fact explains the superiority of the
paleolithic, that is, more ancient drawings, found in
caves, to the neolithic, that is, more recent drawings.
This is a fact passed over altogether or left without
explanation."†

In his fascinating book *At the Edge of History*, William Irwin Thompson joggles the mind with the suggestion, "What if the history of the world is a myth,
but the myth is the remains of the real history of the
earth?

†P. D. Ouspensky, *A New Model of the Universe* (New York: Vintage Books,
1971).

"Whenever it has suited his ideological purposes," he writes, "man has scrupulously destroyed or ignored the record of the past so that its tragedies could not interfere with progress and the ambitions of the present. Voltaire knew what he was talking about when he said, 'History is the lie commonly agreed upon.' . . . If," he points out, "so brilliant a man as David Hume could claim, in his history of England, that no civilization existed in Ireland before the Normans conquered it (when in fact it was Irish scholars Charlemagne called upon when he wished the end of the Dark Ages and founded the Holy Roman Empire), why should we think that we are now immune to the same ethno-centric ignorance and blindness? Consciously or unconsciously most of our Meso-American historians avoid the pieces of information that would unsettle their world views."‡

It is difficult to forget, after all, that Homer's Troy was once considered a myth by all the reputable scholars, historians, and archaeologists of the nineteenth century. A chap named Heinrich Schliemann was regarded with vast amusement for believing that Troy must actually exist outside the pages of the *Iliad* and could be dug up. Schliemann went out and made a fortune, which he spent on searching for Troy, and he found it. He wasn't even a trained archaeologist.

Consider, too, the "myth" of survival after death that occupies us. Recently Dr. Elizabeth Kubler-Ross

‡William Irwin Thompson, *At the Edge of History* (New York: Harper & Row, 1971).

has been interviewing people who came very near to death, or who actually died medically and were returned to life. The results of her research have been fascinating, and have gained much attention. The people she interviewed described having the same experience with almost uncanny similarity. They spoke of leaving their bodies, of hovering at some distance above the bed on which their bodies lay. A few were even able to describe in detail what the doctors and nurses looked like who rushed to the bedside, and what was said and what was done. Without exception they recalled sensations of great peacefulness and of a deep serenity.

The curious point I'd like to add here—without in any way denigrating this—is that in ancient books of mysticism one can read these same descriptions of the dying experience, and in exactly the same words. These descriptions have lain there, however, labeled as myth or fantasy, awaiting a twentieth-century scientific mind to give them respectability for us. Ten years ago, for instance, I listened to a tape in which a man described this "out-of-body" experience before being brought back to life after heart failure. The tape was circulated by a very intelligent group of people on an almost underground basis because they didn't wish to be thought "strange."

Pyramids. Stonehenge. Ancient cultures. Medicine men. Extrasensory perception. In an unerring pursuit of what can be seen and grasped we may have lost as much as we have gained. We may have chosen the wrong path into the labyrinth and barred ourselves from reaching the heart of the maze. "There are more things in heaven and earth, Horatio, than are dreamt of in your philosophy."

For myself, I believe that we have lived many lives, and have been traveling through time for longer than we may imagine. It is certainly the only rational explanation to me for the limitations and injustices in life, for if "God is love," then how can we explain the terrible injustices—children born mute, retarded, or crippled, earthquakes that banish thousands in an instant, the good who die young, the prisoner in his cage, the murderer and his victim, the Mozart among us who writes music at the age of three, the child who can solve calculus problems at six—unless this life is but one of many and we are each of us, individually, working out a pattern begun many lives before?

"It is curious that in the West," writes Raynor Johnson, "we have come to accept the Law of Cause and Effect without question in the scientific domain, but seem reluctant to recognize its sway on other levels of significance. Yet every religion teaches this as part of its ethical code: 'Whatsoever a man sows that shall he also reap.' In Oriental philosophy this is the great Law of Karma. Whatsoever a man sows . . . sometime and somewhere the fruits of it will be reaped by him. As a boomerang thrown by a skillful person will move rapidly away to a great distance on a circular path, but finally returns to the hand of the thrower, so there is an inexorable law of justice which runs through the world on all levels. There is no question of rewards and punishments at all: it is simply a question of inevitable consequence, and applies equally to good things and evil things."*

But in this area nothing is provable in the sense that it can ever be physically grasped and known. We are afloat in a world of the invisible, clinging to the familiar and to the tangible, and terrified of the unknown.

But I like what the religious existentialists—the theologians—have to say about this. They present us with the paradox that God can only be found when Man has achieved an inner security and an inner freedom, and when Man no longer looks upon God as a harsh or benevolent parent in Heaven. Why? Because when Man's faith lies securely in himself, they tell us, then he is no longer afraid of the unknown, and being ready at last to face the unknown he meets God. For the Unknown *is* God.

*Raynor C. Johnson, *Imprisoned Splendor* (New York: Harper & Row, 1953).

13

Simplifying

 WHAT I HAD SET OUT TO DO WHEN I moved to ten acres in Nova Scotia was to simplify my life. I had read the Club of Rome report that predicted serious oil shortages two years before the energy crisis of '73, and I wanted to walk softly and to conserve, but I also wanted to reduce the *things* in my life, for this would be freedom, too. Once in a spartan mood I had estimated that the objects I would want to save in case of fire could be placed in one suitcase: a dozen or more prized books of philosophy,*

---

*My editor has suggested that I list these, which would include: *The Fourth Way*, by P. D. Ouspensky; Thoreau's *Walden; Commentaries on the Teachings of Gurdjieff and Ouspensky* (5 volumes), by Maurice Nicoll; *Living Zen*, by Robert Linssen; Emerson's *Essays; Man and Time*, by J. B. Priestley; *The Outsider*, by Colin Wilson; *Man's Search for Meaning*, by Victor Frankl; *At the Edge of History*, by William Irwin Thompson; *The Urgency of Change*, by Krishnamurti; *Man's Emerging Mind*, by N. J. Berrill; *Toward A Psychology of Being*, by Abraham Maslow.

two irreplaceable photograph albums of my sons growing up, a Rumanian silver ikon of which I was fond, and an unusual beer stein I'd bought in a junk shop for five dollars when I was an art student in Philadelphia. Gaining courage from the discovery of what *did* matter to me, I wanted, in moving to East Tumbril, to discard what did not.

This ferocity of purpose was helped enormously by the fact that machines and I are not compatible at all, and regard each other with mutual hostility. I felt that more than enough months of my life had been spent in waiting for service men to come and repair them when they broke down, or at the telephone asking why they did *not* come to repair them when they broke down.

And so no roto-tiller for me, with all those moving parts. Instead I bought a very good wide-mouth shovel, and eventually a pickax for the more stubborn turf, and managed very nicely to dig and turn over the soil: in the spring, before I planted, and in the fall, when I fertilized or turned over a cover crop. As an extra dividend I grew lean and bendable and happily put aside all need to watch calories or to diet.

My tools extended to a wheelbarrow—used so much that I bought a spare—and trowels, which kept breaking, and eventually I added a neat little contrivance called a cultivator, which had a large slender iron wheel plus disc, harrow, and plow attachments, and two wooden handles pushed exclusively by human muscle. With these, and a judicious use of hay to keep down weeds, I was able to grow an abundance of spinach, peas, turnips, corn, tomatoes, zucchini, onions, green and yellow beans, broccoli, potatoes, pepper-mint, dill, comfrey, garlic, and parsley. I saw no reason to change the mix.

Just as Zen defines love by eliminating what it is not, I measured accumulation by its value to this new life. An electric coffee percolator was not essential at all but an empty glass jar had innumerable wonderful uses. So did an empty cardboard carton. Electric yo-gurt makers were redundant when I need only wrap a bowl of yogurt in a blanket and put it aside in an un-used oven. A barrel found on the Far Beach and rolled up the hill to the house could become a rain barrel if I sliced off several inches of drain pipe. An old shallow bureau drawer found in the barn was perfect for sprouting seeds when I filled it with earth.

If the house was somewhat empty at first it filled soon enough with treasures I found out on the Far Beach: a large smooth, round stone with a hole worn in its center from the tides; dozens of whelk shells that I placed on windowsills and heaped in bowls; a beauti-ful three-foot curve of grained wood; old hand-carved lobster buoys, pieces of driftwood, and dried grasses that I hung from the rafters along with onions and herbs. One day I plucked from the shore out by the lighthouse a delicate wild plant that the wind had sealed to the ground and shaped like a fan; I brought it home and hung it on a wall and it was as lovely as any painting. I made root-cellar boxes out of lobster crates, lining them with hardware cloth to keep out mice, and buried one in the ground and covered it with hay; the last of the turnips was still moist in the spring.

In the other crates I planted herbs: basil, sage, oregano, parsley, and chervil.

The dictionary defines "essential" as relating to or constituting essence, and the "individual, real or ultimate nature of a thing" was what I began to learn in East Tumbril. We need far less than we realize. I remember visiting a summer cottage in New England with two British friends a dozen years ago; I remember how Thea exclaimed when she saw two kettles and an old tin dishpan mended with screws sold for this purpose. She said, "We do this in England but I never thought I'd see a kettle mended in America."

America is surrounded by countries that mend old kettles; we are an exception on this planet, not the rule. In Bulgaria what struck me forcibly were the fences the peasants made to confine a sheep or a few chickens: they were woven by hand out of twigs and the slender branches of saplings gathered from the hillsides. They were not only utilitarian but beautifully natural and pleasing to the eye. Those farmers worked with what was at hand, using their ingenuity; it must have taken days to gather the materials and then to weave them into a rough mesh, but it was all they had, and when it was done it was theirs, a work they could look at with pride.

If we are heading into a world of shortages we, too, will have to learn the art of mending and preserving; it will do us no harm and it will sharpen our wits. I have read that in Zen monasteries or schools the first lesson a Zen student must learn is to practice economy in living: lights never burned wastefully, a minimum of utensils, a single mat to sit on; the fewer the number of possessions, the more we are in touch with them and know their nature and care for them.

The new kind of world I was inhabiting began to have a realness for me that no other ever had. I discovered that in a smaller, more natural world there is space for relationship and for contact. Everything becomes important. My eight tomato plants and I went through crisis after crisis the first year; in October when I dug them out of the soil to add to the compost pile I felt I was ending a long and intimate friendship and there were tears in my eyes. Where I lived there were no garden supply houses to sell me organic materials wrapped in shiny sealed bags. When my older son Christopher came for several weeks' vacation in August, we spent a day making forays into the woods for pine needles and rich humus, and then to the beach for muck, which we mixed with sawdust and wood chips from the lumberyard in town. All of these materials fed the earth, and the earth fed the vegetables; everything has its use. When I built a wood fire for warmth I became aware that the wood had reached me by a long process; I had first met it when it was dumped in my yard in the spring, after which I laboriously stacked the three cords piece by piece in the sun for seasoning, and then in the fall—for want of a better arrangement—I carted and moved it piece by piece to the barn for the winter. My neighbor Keith Crowell says there is warm heat and cold heat: I only understood what he meant after adding wood stoves to my life.

There were wild plants, too. I would harvest the

herbs I raised and dry them between screens but I would also gather and dry wild yarrow and red clover for winter tea. In the fall the primroses were heavy with rose hips and I picked them and simmered them on the stove, then strained them, combined them with apple juice, and had a wonderful free vitamin-C breakfast drink. I picked orach out on the Far Beach and cooked it or ate it raw in a salad. But perhaps most surprising of all to me was the discovery one day that except for college tuitions I had lived for a year on less than three thousand dollars, without trying to, and without any noticeable moderation at all. Nature had supplied the abundance and most of my recreation as well.

In living with less clutter in a life the mind also becomes less cluttered; in peeling away accumulation and getting to the core of matters I was also peeling away outgrown habits and emotions and reactions, but above all I was being taught to appreciate, to "grasp the nature, worth, quality, or significance" of small things. Appreciation is surely an underestimated emotion: I would feel it when I walked into a warm house after a cold hour on the beach, or when I discovered a good book to read and deliberately slowed my pace to make it last; when I sat down to a beef stew with all the vegetables in it picked from my garden only a few hours earlier in the day, or when a friend brought a lobster, or stopped in to chat on a snowy evening.

Appreciation of small things was what I felt most of all when the Groundhog Day storm of 1976 arrived, and I discovered, not without astonishment, that after two winters I had become prepared at last. It was a fiendish, record-breaking storm that no meteorologists had seen coming; it struck with hurricane force, the waves pouring over the Far Beach into the pond and changing its topography forever. When the wind finished with us twenty-four hours later there were lobster boats sitting atop wharfs, trailers without roofs, electric poles lying around like jackstraws, trees down along the roads, and for days the electricity would pop on and off because of the salt spray shorting the lines. But for this occasion I had thick plywood storm shutters to fasten across the largest window; I had an Ashley stove with a thermostat, and a wood-burning cookstove as well. For water I tied ropes to the handles of buckets and lowered them into the well outside. I had a sufficiency of candles and kerosene lamps. I went to bed in all my clothes, with blankets under and over me, and when the fire in the Ashley died out at four in the morning and the cold woke me up, I started a fire in the kitchen cookstove, made a cup of hot cocoa, and sat down at the kitchen table to watch the sun rise pink and golden in the east. I have never appreciated a sunrise more. Or a cup of hot cocoa. Or a warm fire.

"It's not the barrenness of an empty room or an empty life that we seek," Robert Henri has written. "We would get rid of clutter and thus get room for fullness."†

---

†Robert Henri, *The Art Spirit* (Philadelphia: J. B. Lippincott, 1960).

14

Reflections

 I HAVE COME TO REALIZE A CURIOUS truth about myself, living here alone. Slowly I begin to understand that my whole life has been based on anger and rebellion, which at times must surely have engendered some amazing resentments and even hatreds: a startling insight for one who thought herself nonviolent, even gentle. I look back on the usual difficult childhood and remember the psychiatrist saying that my rebellions had preserved me, had in effect saved my life, that when a child is faced with insoluble dilemmas, anger is healthier than submission or giving up. But anger and rebellion have ruled my life ever since. I have never learned who I am without it.

Some anger is good: it's what made me fight a

doubtful prognosis when a member of my family was ill for months. It's what kept me writing when my life was all steaming formulas and wet diapers ("Of course she'll give up her writing once she has a child"). But my rebelliousness went so deep that, faced with a can of asparagus that instructed me to OPEN AT THIS END, I always, stubbornly, opened it at the other.

Now, suddenly, there is no anger *against*, and there is no one to fight *for* . . . except myself. I realize I have come to the largest responsibility of all: myself. Not in the selfish, ego-centered sense, but in the most literal interpretation of the word: response-to-myself. It feels a very small and puny confrontation after those more glorious battles.

Living alone is a learning process but most of all it's an unlearning process. For one thing living with others is easier. On the simplest, most elementary basis it's easier because fewer decisions are necessary. When a woman, for instance, gets up in the morning and is not alone she will say, "What would you like for breakfast?" or "What time will you be home today?" and the replies to this subtly alter her day and sometimes her mood. When we rise alone we have to decide our own mood for that day, and our own plans; we even have to decide between cornflakes or an egg.

I may or may not live alone for the rest of my life but I am learning a great deal from it. I am more vulnerable alone, just as the single tree on my ten acres is more vulnerable than the tree hidden in the forest. I am more susceptible to rejection and to self-pity, and to emotions that companions would persuade me out of, or challenge. But if I do not panic, if I remember that I was born with none of these deficiencies, then I can begin to toss out the excess baggage of negatives until I am no longer heavy with their densities but light, buoyant, transparent, and emotions pass through me without lingering. When we can do this we are no longer alone, I think, because we have cut our way through the thicket to ourselves.

I'm working on it.

Tao says, "In the pursuit of learning, every day something is acquired. In the pursuit of Tao, every day something is dropped."

I have been rereading Gabriel Marcel's *Mystery of Being*. I come to these two paragraphs which reflect, in their turn, the ultimate loneliness in living, and one of its deepest joys. "We can," he writes, "have a very strong feeling that somebody who is sitting in the same room as ourselves . . . someone whom we can look at and listen to and whom we could touch if we wanted . . . is nevertheless further away from us than some loved one who is perhaps thousands of miles away or perhaps, even, no longer among the living. We could say that the man sitting beside us was in the same room as ourselves, but that he was not really *present* there, that his presence did not make itself felt . . . One might say that what we have with this person . . . is communication without communion: he understands what I say to him, but he does not understand *me*.

"The opposite phenomenon, however, can also take

place. When somebody's presence does really make itself felt it can refresh my inner being; it reveals me to
myself, it makes me more fully aware than I should be
if I were not exposed to its impact."*

There is no such thing as loss, really, only change.
We set fire to a birch log and the fire consumes it and
we have irrevocably lost our birch log but now we have
wood ash, which is composed of potash, potassium,
carbon, and other rich vegetable matter.

Euripides said, "Who knows but life be that which
men call death, and death what men call life?" I like
this. I picture myself about to die. I don't want to
leave but my time is up, my span completed. I say
goodbye, clinging a little to those people I've loved
and enjoyed, I fill my eyes for a last time with the
incredible colors and beauty around me, and as I brace
myself and begin the struggle of letting go I feel the
darkness sweep over me, I'm precipitated through a
long dark tunnel into a bright light that blinds me,
hands roughly handle me, I cry out in protest and hear
a voice exclaim, "It's a girl, Mrs. G., you've just given
birth to a healthy baby girl," and I have entered what
we call life.

When I catch myself feeling sorry for myself I can
feel the resistance, even the outrage at relinquishing
such a rich, lush emotion: it gives a wonderful, spur-
ious sense of being alive. Ouspensky says that self-pity

*Gabriel Marcel, *The Mystery of Being* (Chicago: Henry Regnery Co., 1960).

is the most entertaining negative emotion we can in-
dulge in, and the hardest with which to part.

I believe that everything has its own season, and
each hour its law. If something anticipated arrives too
late it finds us numb, wrung out from waiting, and we
feel—nothing at all. The best things arrive on time.

Jonathan has sent an article entitled "What Do I
Really Want to Do?" It's lovely. I discover that I
should cut a path through the tall grass to the raspberry bushes, I *should* bake bread, I *should* answer
two letters on my desk, but what I really want to do is
walk out to the lighthouse and see if yesterday's storm
washed up any new treasures on the Far Beach.

Camus has written that artists and criminals are the
outcasts of society; after a letter today from J., I
wonder if single women might not be included in this
list. Where, she wonders, can she possibly fit in? She
encloses, too, an interview with Liv Ullmann in the
New York Times, who is quoted as saying that "the
pressure for a woman not to live alone—or to be
alone—is great . . . If they do decide to be alone, part
of their loneliness will come from outside, rather than
inside. Society will pity them, look down on them."†
When Ms. Ullmann dines alone in a restaurant she

†*New York Times*, January 29, 1975.

chooses an out-of-the-way corner and buries her head in a book.

I cannot understand women who look with distaste at the women's movement; my God, I think, where have they been? I look at them with the same curiosity and speculation with which I regard black soldiers in Rhodesia's white army who hunt and kill their black brothers. I can explain it, I can see it, but I cannot understand it.

Small wounds of womanhood:

A husband saying reproachfully, "But you shouldn't *want* to do anything I don't want to do."

A three-hour wait at the dentist's and the dentist explaining later, "I hope you don't mind my taking Mr. X first, without an appointment, but he had a job to get back to."

Overheard at a dinner: Husband: "Give it to Elsie to do, she has time for that sort of thing," Elsie having three preschool children, a house to look after, meals to cook, laundry to do, chauffeuring, and an ageing mother-in-law living with them.

A small-town entrepreneur some years ago hearing the sound of my typewriter, knocking on the door of our apartment, and telling me he needed some typing done.

"I'm working on a book," I tell him. "The typing I'm doing is for myself."

He looks blank. "But these are the reports of twelve

meetings, you could finish them in only three or four days, and I'll pay you a few dollars, too."

"You don't type?" I ask.

"Of course I type," he says indignantly, "but my time's too valuable for this sort of thing."

Or that ubiquitous query when a single woman orders merchandise and gives her name: *"And your husband's name?"*

"No husband," I say, and receive a pitying glance that always makes me want to add brightly, "Eaten by cannibals, you see, when he landed on a desert island after a hurricane swamped his rowboat." Once—but this was *very* nasty—I gave them my husband's name, and after it had been laboriously written down, complete with address, I added innocently, "Since we've been divorced for many years would you like my address now, too?"

But when I feel I've been growing *really* slack I rouse myself and apply for a charge account or a credit card. I have discovered there is nothing more ominous —in the United States, at least—than to be (1) a woman and (2) single and (3) self-employed, and so I can count on an engrossing battle of wits that will last for months and result in a voluminous correspondence.

From *Sex and Society*, by Kenneth Walker and Peter Fletcher: "The sexual act is a form of speech, discourse, dialogue and, like every other means of human communication, its value depends on whether the protagonists have anything to say worth saying."

To be alone is always to risk loneliness but sometimes we feel lonely because we're told we *must* be lonely if we separate ourselves for a moment from the crowd. In her book *Lonely in America*, Suzanne Gordon writes that "in a society whose financial and social coffers are always supposed to be full, loneliness or emotional emptiness is more than emotionally distressing—it's socially stigmatic.... Loneliness equals failure; having people around equals success.... The association between failure, loneliness and solitude is so strong in our culture that people often find it difficult to believe that there are some who like being by themselves."‡

Canada is a gentler country, and different in this sense: coming in tired one evening from too many hours of digging in the garden, I determine to sprawl out and watch whatever CBC television—the only channel I get—is providing that night from eight to nine o'clock. I turn it on, sit down, and proceed to watch—in what is called prime time in the United States—an hour-long program on penguins.

15

The Garden/Summer

 ALONG THE OCEAN'S SHORE THE SEA-
sons are less defined; there's no turning
of foliage to mark the autumn because
the trees are evergreens—pine, fir, and spruce—and
September and October are Nova Scotia's most glorious months. There is a shortening of days and the occasional early-morning frost, no more; there are still
blueberries in the hollows, and blackberries, and the
meadow is lush with rose hips and then suddenly it's
November, about which the old-timers say, "No stars,
no sun, no moon, November." But November can also
resemble March, and March feel like October, and
there will come a fog-wrapped June day that looks and
feels exactly like a foggy day in January. Edward the
postmaster says this is why Nova Scotians live so long:

there are no extremes for the body to adjust to, just a gradual swing of the pendulum between five degrees and seventy-five. No heat waves. No cold waves. Just wind.

But in March there are subtle signs of the earth stirring out of its winter drowsiness. There may be ice on the beach but very thin ice that breaks underfoot with a tinkling sound. The lobster boats venture out again with a fresh load of pots to drop. The sunsets grow intense: purest gold turning in minutes to vivid pink, or a sweep of sherbet colors—lemon, orange, raspberry. Fading into a cold twilight, it leaves the earth the color of Concord grapes against a blue, silver-white water; against this the lights of the returning lobster boats glow like gold.

Or there are brilliant crisp days when the whitecaps in the harbor match the frosty clear white of a sea gull's wings. There will be fog, too, soft, mysterious, blurring sharp edges and good to feel on one's skin, like fine misty spray. One day I walked over to the Far Beach, curious about the loudness of the surf on such a quiet fogbound morning. The waves came to me out of the mist, a series of small ones followed by two roaring combers that swept up the beach to my feet. As they retreated, all the rocks and stones and pebbles over which they ebbed made a wonderful sound, like applause, nudging each other, moving, clinking, adjusting themselves against the pull of the tide.

A red tulip suddenly appeared in my garden, followed by a purple one. And suddenly it was April, and the sound of pinkwinks could be heard from the bogs at night. It was time to start planting.

When I came to Nova Scotia I had never gardened before; nothing had prepared me for the most absorbing, exciting, and consuming work I'd ever tried. In what other job can a person be inventor, scientist, landscape gardener, ditch digger, researcher, problem solver, artist, exorcist, and on top of all that eat one's successes at dinner?

I love a good fight—life is tame enough these days —and here was an adversary who played by no rules and who seemed—Nature being what she is, completely, utterly neutral—to do everything possible to prevent humans from growing food and yet, paradoxically, insists on producing under the most discouraging conditions. She has designed slugs and flea beetles and cabbage maggots and hornworms, and if one battles these with diligence, then she will send a month of drought, or of fog and rain, just to keep one humble. What continues to astonish me about a garden is that you can walk past it in a hurry, see something wrong, stop to set it right, and emerge an hour or two later breathless, contented, and wondering what on earth happened. A garden germinates not only seeds but ideas; it's pure creation. It smells so good, too.

Into my garden soil—heavy and claylike—went lobster shells and fish bones and potato skins and orange rinds and eggshells, wood ash, lime, bone meal, and above all seaweed: seaweed heaped first on a drying frame I built until the sun and wind turned it brittle and hard as wire, or seaweed stacked in piles that by spring had settled into a delicious jellylike mush. "You can tell a real garden by the worms and the birds," Bobby says, and he was right: the earthworms in my gardens grew fat and sleek because there were no chemicals to hurt them or the soil, and in turn they drew the birds that fed on the nastier insects; each morning when I opened the door there would be a rush of wings as the birds left the garden.

Nicole brought me an old Irish saying as a gift: "Earth without stones is like flesh without bones," and certainly the largest crop I grew was stones. With practice, however, I found I could dig out quite large rocks with a heavy thin metal rod discovered in the barn. I'd hammer it under the rock, then sit on it or stamp on it, and eventually it would prise the rock from its hole. I grew to know the former tenants very well by the objects I dug out of the earth when I made new beds: pottery and china shards, which I kept for pots, rusted horseshoes, and I must have dug out enough rusty spikes and nails to fill a dozen buckets.

Plant north by south, my neighbors told me, and I did, except for the spinach, but it didn't matter to the slugs which way the rows went. In other climates and places gardens may be raided by raccoons and wood-chucks or deer: in East Tumbril it's slugs, an invasion of them after every heavy rain, and in the spring it rains a lot. I have nothing against snails in general. A periwinkle, for instance, belongs to the snail family, of the marine variety. It lives in a small round shell, in circumference about the size of a thumbnail, and it's decorated enchantingly in spirals of brown, black, beige, and red. It clings to the rocks so tenaciously it looks cemented there, but I've seen them move. It's a double-take affair...sunning myself on a rock, I would look down into the water beside me and say, "There's kelp and there's rockweed and there's a periwinkle on the edge of that rock," and then a few minutes later the periwinkle is no longer on the edge, and peering closer, I see tiny stick-like legs in motion; I realize he's hurrying off somewhere on business at *his* speed, which, considering the fact that I'm seated contemplating the world, is faster than mine.

A periwinkle is decorative and edible, too, when steamed like escargot, and so it is useful as well as appealing. A slug is a member of the land-snail family, but I have gone so far as to ask God for enlightenment as to what He had in mind when He created him. A slug is thick and fat and pale; he gorges on tender young plants and grows thicker and fatter. The organic way of dealing with him is to place a pie tin at ground level in the garden and fill it with beer, which slugs love, and in which they blissfully drown themselves.

I bought beer and aluminum pie plates, and then I bought more beer and more aluminum pie plates. I began to feel that the garbage pickup man must suspect me of being an alcoholic; I began to picture slugs converging on my garden from miles up the road. When my beer bill reached fifteen dollars I conferred with Bobby about the native remedy. This was salt, and eminently practical because at the fishing co-op down the road it was free: the flakes and beads of coarse salt with which they preserve haddock, cod, and herring were dumped outside in snowy piles, to be shoveled into buckets by anyone determined enough to come and get it. I hauled this back and distributed it, and after this, each June, my gardens looked like tennis courts with thick white lines defining them. The salt never seemed to hurt the earthworms or the vegetables inside the lines, it lasted through several rains, and kept the slugs at bay. Barely.

At the beginning I knew very little, and would keep running to my books for answers. I even had to ask where and how the fruit would appear on a tomato plant and one evening when Frank stopped in to see my garden I proudly showed him my corn, just appearing aboveground in tender shoots. He took a long look, grinned, and told me it was as handsome a row of chickweed as he'd seen in a long time.

But knowing so little brought surprise after surprise: the way broccoli grows, designed by some celestial order to send out great leaves, and then at last a tiny cluster in the center that grows and grows until it's the size of a basketball; the dark green curling leaves of spinach, ruffled like curtains; the fantastic horn-shaped orange flowers of the zucchini, with its two different kinds of leaves; the silky tassels of corn, the fragrance of English lavender and basil and sage. And for all this I had planted only one seed, microscopic in size, and then another and another.

I shouldn't care to be a farmer with hundreds of acres to plant and harvest; I'd miss the miracles and the knowingness. I grew five pepper plants in pots indoors, and when I transplanted them outside they didn't thrive. I transplanted them again to a richer corner, placed a barbed-wire cage around them, and secured a sheet of transparent plastic to it with clothespins. By mid-September they had just begun to flower, too late a triumph but we had both tried hard and learned. After the rains stopped in June there came a month-long drought and the wells sank dangerously low all over the village. I read about farmers in the Midwest losing acre after acre of crops but my two rain barrels watered the gardens for a week and after that I saved laundry and bath water and carried it to the plants in buckets.

And then there were the herbs. I think if I were starting life all over again I would have to become an herbalist. When I first began reading about them I would disappear for hours from the world in every sense but the physical. I've learned now to limit my forays; I confine myself to small nibbles and ingest them slowly. It's not just the history of herbs, or their constituents, or the use that's been made of them for thousands of years; it's the catching a glimpse of something larger behind them, like being aware of movement in a corner of the room and turning one's head too slowly to catch it.

Take, for instance, the piquant little coincidence that Mrs. Grieve—she calls herself Mrs. M. Grieve—notes in Volume One of her *A Modern Herbal*. "The flower of the skullcap, one of the best cures for insomnia," she writes "has a strong resemblance to the shape of the human skull ... the little blue flower of Eyebright with its yellow center that suggests the human

eye is so useful for tired eyes that the French have
called it 'casse lunettes' . . . the flowers of many of the
herbs which purify the blood are red, e.g. Scarlet Pim-
pernel, Burdock, red clover . . . most of the flowers
used for jaundice are yellow, like the Dandelion, Agri-
mony, Celandine, Hawkweed and Marigold . . . the medicinal value of Nettles is indicated by their sting: they
are used internally to stimulate circulation."*

Apparently Nature has a sense of humor, as well as
considerable doubt about our perceptiveness; she gives
a few clues to nudge us.

If you find this a modest coincidence consider the
herb foxglove, a plant that is as lethal as a bomb and
yet saves lives every hour of the day. Its leaves contain
four stimulants: digitoxin, digitalin, digitalein, and di-
gitonin, from which our digitalis is made. "If, however,
Digitalis fails to act on the heart as desired," Mrs.
Grieve notes, "Lily-of-the-valley may be substituted
and will often be found of service."

A backup system. Very efficient.

I look up rosemary to learn the type of soil it
prefers. Gerard's *Herball* says of it, "The Arabians and
other Pysistions succeeding, do write, that Rosemary
comforteth the braine, the memorie, the inward
senses, and restoreth speech unto them that are pos-
sessed with the dumb palsie . . . and, eaten comforts
the heart and makes it merry, quickens the spirits and
make them more lively."

*Mrs. M. Grieve, *A Modern Herbal* (New York: Hafner Publishing Co.,
1971).

Its name means dew of the sea—Ros Marinus—
which is surely enough in itself to "comfort the heart
and quicken the spirits." But there is myth and history
here, too. Anne of Cleves wore a wreath of rosemary
at her wedding—could it be coincidence that she was
the one who survived marriage to Henry the VIII? Sir
Thomas More wrote of it being "sacred to remem-
brance and therefore to friendship." It's been used to
flavor ale and wine. The Spaniards revere it as one of
the bushes that gave shelter to the Virgin Mary on her
flight into Egypt. Many herbalists consider it the best
cure-all among all the herbs. In French hospitals it was
customary for years to burn rosemary with juniper
berries to purify the air and prevent infections. It's a
tonic, astringent, diaphoretic, and stimulant. One ancient writer said of it, "Make thee a box of the wood of
Rosemary and smell of it and it shall preserve thy
youth."

But then there is also the lowly green parsley that
we absently push aside when it garnishes our dinner
plate. It contains 22,500 units of vitamin A per ounce,
its iron content surpasses that of spinach, and it contains five times as much vitamin C as an equal weight
of oranges. It also contains potassium, calcium, phosphorus, and vitamin B_1.

Or try eating a violet, both flowers and leaves, instead of making a bouquet of it. In *Stalking the
Healthful Herbs*, Euell Gibbons tells us that violets are
so rich in vitamin C that they have to be approached
with a very real caution. Mrs. Grieve devotes five en-
cyclopedic pages to the violet. "They were used by the

Athenians to 'moderate anger,' to procure sleep and 'to comfort and strengthen the heart.' Pliny prescribes a liniment of violets and vinegar for gout and disorder of the spleen ... The ancient Britons used the flowers as a cosmetic, and in a Celtic poem they are recommended to be employed steeped in goats' milk to increase female beauty." The violet is also, I might add, one of a number of herbs that is being tested as a possible cure for, or inhibitor of, cancer.

There are names of herbs that are weird and marvelous: Devil's Bit Scabrous, for instance, or Cuckoo-Pint, and Viper's Bugloss. Or how about Lady's Bedstraw, or something called Burnet Saxifrage or Sassy Bark or Common Polypody?

I had to choose among all these herbs. I made small plantings of basil, sage, rosemary, chervil, Italian parsley, and oregano, but I concentrated above all on comfrey and planted twenty-one roots three feet apart from each other, happily giving up half a garden to them. I settled upon comfrey as a specialty because I could eat comfrey as a vegetable, drink it as a healthful, soothing tea, bind up a bloody cut with it or use its roots as a poultice for burns or insect bites, feed it to chickens, goats, geese, or sheep if I ever acquired them, and use its leftovers in the garden as a nitrogen-rich compost. It's a cell-proliferant, demulcent, and astringent; its mucilagelike substance, allantoin, speeds healing. For livestock it has twice the protein of alfalfa, and its nutrients are more digestible. Its roots go down into the earth eight or ten feet and so it can withstand any drought, and it can be grown in almost any climate. A medical journal of the year 1528 said of it, "The rootes are goode if they be broken and dronken for them that spitte bloode and are goode to glewe together fresh wounds."

One day I thought to try and "glewe together a wound" with it. Mine was an old and stubborn wound: a deep cut on a finger that dishwashing and gardening kept from healing. I brought out a dried comfrey leaf, rubbed it into a powder, and sprinkled it on a wet bandage that I wrapped around my finger. The bandage floated away in the morning's dishwater and I forgot about the experiment until three nights later I found myself admiring an artistic, strange white scar on my tanned finger, and wondered where it had come from. Amazed, I realized this was all that was left of my stubborn, angry red cut.

I wonder: can anyone rationally suggest there is no order to the universe when there are such small potent miracles as herbs abroad?

16

A New Kind of Country

The man who goes alone can start today; but
he who travels with another must wait 'til that
other is ready.

—THOREAU

 AND SO EACH SEASON HAS ITS TURN.
Between drying herbs and eating and
freezing vegetables and observing and
watering and picking and weeding, a summer in East
Tumbril goes by in a blaze of sun and abundance. My
ten acres, flat and scrubby to the eye, produced a
wealth of berries for desserts, all the vegetables I could
eat, salad greens, good spring water, herbs for winter
teas, and sometimes such a joy that I would stand still
and gasp, "But what if I had never come here? What if
I had waited for someone to do this with, and never
done it at all?"

This dream at least I had carried out, and it was
mine. And in a curious way it drew me very close to—
and reconnected me with—someone I'd lost touch

125

with a long time ago: the child who had dreamed it. It was good to meet her again and say, "You see? To grow up is not necessarily to forget; a promise has been kept."

By late August I discovered that I had begun to acquire a past in East Tumbril. Escaping the garden for an hour, I would walk out to the Far Beach and remember the more leisurely visits in winter when life was less hectic. I would smile at the strips of white cloth I'd hung on alder bushes a year ago to mark the blueberries I'd found nearby. I could imagine a new generation of minnows in the little tidal pond between the rocks. A pattern had begun to emerge. I would think, "But I remember that in November (or March or December) the harbor had looked so," and there had been wind, hadn't there? My thoughts begun to turn to stacking firewood under cover in the barn and to fertilizing gardens and putting them to bed for the winter under hay and seaweed. It would soon be time, too, to visit the islanders again before the weather changed. Nicole had gone—arrivals and departures again—but I'd heard that two new Americans from Florida had moved in down the road to begin home-steading.

The real seasons of the year are not marked by the calendar, but in the completion of this cycle there was a deep sense of rhythm, of ebb and flow, a feeling of everything dovetailing and fitting together such as I'd never experienced before, so that I came to see how society contrives to rob us of a friendship with the earth and its seasons. Or perhaps it was even simpler than this; perhaps it was what my neighbor Ann Lee said when she first viewed the great sweep of harbor and sky from my window: "You must feel very close to God here."

Nothing in life stands still. The tides are in incessant motion, the earth moves on its axle, our bodies manufacture twenty million new blood cells every second, and yesterday's mistakes are forgivable because this is today.... I changed a great deal from living in East Tumbril, outwardly as well as inwardly. One day when my son Jonathan visited me in February and the pipes froze he said, "How calm you are! Do you remember how this would have upset you three years ago in New Jersey?" On a visit back to the States a friend said, "You look so different now, so relaxed, the strain's gone from your eyes."

Some of the time and space of the Nova Scotia coast is inside of me now and always will be: it is the best part, and the newest.

What did I learn? I learned to fashion a day out of nothing at all and to give it shape and balance. I learned how to make a blueberry pie, to be very quiet and watch birds circling and tomatoes ripening. I learned how to work hard physically, to sickle grass, haul earth, dig holes and trenches, fight slugs, and cultivate a garden. I made new friends, and one of them was myself. I learned the hours of the day and the seasons of the year in a sense completely new to me, and I learned about wind and storms and droughts and harvests.

I learned this, too: that we are each, inside of us, a

country with our own mountains and plateaus and chasms and storms and seas of tranquility but like a Third World country we remain largely unexplored, and sometimes even impoverished, for want of a little investment.

One early June day in East Tumbril I walked out to the Far Beach to pick some orach, which grows among the rocks out there by the water. It was a day when the harbor was so calm and so exactly the color of the cloudless sky that St. Ann's Point seemed to float suspended in the air, and a dory rounding the point looked as if it was heading straight into the sky. I could never decide whether I loved sun or fog the better in East Tumbril. Each had its magic: pointed evergreens rising out of the mist like shapes veiled behind a curtain, images blurred like those in a remembered dream, the fog soft and ghostly, a silent world seen through clouded glass. Or this radiance of gold splinters on sapphire. Silver versus gold.

I gathered orach in the sun, and coming back with my basket filled I saw a car parked at the end of Lighthouse Road: the first tourists of the season, an Illinois license plate. In my fishing boots and blue jeans, a scarf tied over my head, I was a native; I would have smiled, said hello, and walked past them but the man asked if the path to the lighthouse was private or open to the public. I assured him gravely that it was perfectly acceptable to walk to the lighthouse.

"What have you got there?" asked his wife, seeing the green leaves in the basket.

"Orach," I told her. I was already nibbling on a leaf

and I offered some to her and the children. "It tastes like spinach, with a flavor of salt air. I picked it to cook for dinner."

Questions suddenly began to pour out of them. They'd arrived only that morning on the ferry to the south of us, fresh from the United States, and they wondered about the wooden boxes piled everywhere, and at the boats drawn up on the beach; they wondered if the beach pond was man-made, and why ther were so many boards piled up high out near the lighthouse.

I told them that the beach pond had been formed by Nature—by the wind and the tides—and not by Man. The pile of boards, I explained, had been brought there yesterday by truck to be delivered to two Americans living on an island nearby. When the tide rose in the pond Brad Gaullet would bring in his boat, float the lumber out to it, load it on deck, and reverse the process when he reached the island. I told them that the lobster season had ended on this coast just two days ago, that the boats were dry-docked for the summer and the boxes were lobster pots, retired now, too, for the season.

"Not traps?" asked the man quickly.

"They're called pots here," I said.

They thanked me and climbed out of the car to begin the walk to the lighthouse, the children racing ahead.

I lingered a moment, looking after them, and it occurred to me how meaningless the scene must look to someone who didn't know. A beach pond at low tide.

A lighthouse that resembled an Erector Set. A pile of boards stacked high on the shore. Three boats propped up out of reach of the tides. Dozens of weather-beaten wooden pots in rows.

You had to realize, I thought, that everything here had a story behind it, a purpose, a history, a reason for being. Like the tidal pond that lies empty and serene in the sun until a pebble ripples its surface and discloses the infinite life within.

Otherwise it was just another village and another beach on the long drive up the coast to Halifax.

ABOUT THE AUTHOR

DOROTHY GILMAN is the author of several popular Mrs. Pollifax novels. She divides her time between New Mexico and Nova Scotia.